THE ARCHANGEL'S GIFT

DICK MORGAN

ILLUSTRATIONS BY STEPHEN ADAMS

Copyright © 2022 Dick Morgan.

All rights reserved. No part of this book may be reproduced, stored, or transmitted by any means—whether auditory, graphic, mechanical, or electronic—without written permission of both publisher and author, except in the case of brief excerpts used in critical articles and reviews. Unauthorized reproduction of any part of this work is illegal and is punishable by law.

ISBN: 979-8-88640-235-3 (sc)
ISBN: 979-8-88640-236-0 (hc)
ISBN: 979-8-88640-237-7 (e)

Because of the dynamic nature of the Internet, any web addresses or links contained in this book may have changed since publication and may no longer be valid. The views expressed in this work are solely those of the author and do not necessarily reflect the views of the publisher, and the publisher hereby disclaims any responsibility for them.

One Galleria Blvd., Suite 1900, Metairie, LA 70001
1-888-421-2397

For my wife and daughter,
who opened my heart for me;
still warm from their embrace,
i love all i see.

Jamie received a strange gift on Christmas Eve

CHAPTER 1

THREE QUESTIONS

Jamie Mayer's dad believed in angels. He said that he'd met one once, and they'd had a remarkably fine conversation. He refused to speak of it further however, saying with a wink that such events were personal. Jamie herself didn't know how she felt about angels. After all, she knew that parents sometimes tricked their kids into believing things just for the fun of it. All she knew for certain was that every year, as Christmas time approached, her father went nuts.

Jamie's dad was just a regular guy most of the time—a man who worked at home doing amazing and complicated things on the computer in the basement, for which he received "the big bucks," as he called it. And most of the time, Jamie's dad liked regular-guy sorts of things: old John Wayne movies, Superbowl Sunday, tinkering with things that had motors in them, and the ultimate regular guy mystery, the *Saturday Night Fights*. But by Thanksgiving, all of that dropped away like leaves from an October tree, and he transformed into something between a book-thumping Professor Christmas and an elfin child who refused to grow up.

It began the day after Thanksgiving, actually. The angels appeared first. Jamie would find them staring back at her from cross-stitched wall hangings in the entry way as she took off her raincoat. Then they would appear as bendable figures perched atop the hallway mirror, looking at her as she combed her hair. Soon they appeared as centerpieces holding candles above her plate as she ate, and as tiny crystal suspensions in the kitchen window that gleamed in her eyes as she put away the clean silverware. She would find magazine prints of angels carefully cut out and taped to the wall just opposite the toilet in the bathroom. There was no getting away from them.

By the first of December, the other decorations began to emerge. Red and green poinsettias, candles, and evergreen boughs sprouted like weeds throughout the house. By the time the Christmas tree was placed by the front room window, Jamie would find angels, Santas, elves, nutcrackers, reindeer, and snowmen staring back at her everywhere she looked. Even the tablecloth, the pillows, and the welcome mat were replaced with festive red and green stand-ins. During the last few days before Christmas, Jamie would watch her father as he stood in the middle of the living room sipping his hot spiced cider and looking for one more spot to stuff an angel, an elf, or elongated star.

But Christmas music on the radio was the worst. Her dad loved to sing along at the top of his lungs. And although she had to admit her dad had a passable singing voice, she prayed that none of her friends would be over for a visit when her dad happened to take the lead tenor part in Handel's

Messiah, which he loved dearly. After all, she *was* almost nine years old.

Jamie was a slender string of a girl, a platinum haired third grader who had grown legs that seemed too long for her body, like a geranium under a grow-light. She had a button nose full of freckles and always wore her hair in a pony-tail so she could nibble on the end of it when she fretted. At Christmas time, the tip of it was always a little wet.

Thank goodness it was Christmas Eve, and they probably wouldn't be having any friends over at this late hour. In fact, Jamie had already dressed for bed. She was wearing her favorite long white nightgown, and clutching her ever-present sky blue baby blanket (which she called her "cuddly") to her cheek for comfort. Her older sister, Lindsey, lay sprawled across the entire sofa, listening to a song on her CD player. Jamie's mom was still away at the hospital, working the night shift as a nurse. Her dad was rearranging the Christmas tree ornaments again. Suddenly he held up a hand as though to wave, and then stood motionless.

"Hal-le-lu-jah! Hal-le-lu-jah!"

Handel's *Messiah* had come on the radio again, and Jamie's dad was following along in perfect harmony, but at the top of his lungs. Jamie rolled her eyes.

"*Jeez-o-leez*, Dad!" Jamie sighed. "Every time that comes on the radio, you act so…so…" She couldn't think of just the right word, so she sat down by the Christmas tree and put her half of the candy cane back into her mouth. Hers was the curved part; Lindsey had gotten the straight part. Older sisters got the best of everything.

"Did you know that the slang word *Jeez* is probably short for the name *Jesus*?" her dad said through that ever-present holiday grin of his. He took a sip of cider from his mug. Jamie was always astonished that he never spilled it when he sang.

"I think it's short for chill out, Dad," Lindsey said, holding her straight candy-cane half as if it were a cigarette. Lindsey had her earphones on and her eyes closed. She was bucking and gyrating to music that obviously had a more contemporary beat than *Messiah*.

"That was my part in the youth choir at church when I was about your age," Jamie's dad said in Lindsey's general direction. "I can still hit the high notes, too!"

Lindsey, who was continuously snapping her fingers to the music in her ear, said, "Cool, Dad, but *shhh!* I'm like, listening to *my* music now." She took a lick of her candy-cane half and closed her eyes again.

"Let's open some presents!" Jamie said, eyeing one in particular. She picked up a large green-wrapped box from under the tree. She already knew it was for her, and it was just the size of the lap-top computer she so *desperately* wanted. She shook it, listening for the tell-tale clicks of plastic against metal. Nothing.

Jamie's dad frowned. "Presents are for Christmas morning. The real Christmas is Christmas Eve," he said. "Besides, we ought to wait for your mother."

"Aw, come on, Dad!" Jamie pleaded. "Please? She won't mind just *one!*"

"I'll think about it," he answered. "But first, we're going to read the Christmas story. Turn down the radio. Lindsey, off with the earphones."

"Aw, *jeez*, Dad! Every year you do this!" Lindsey said, rolling her eyes. "Like, we've heard it already!"

"So you think you know it pretty well, ay?" Her dad paused, gazing at the two of them and taking small sips from his mug. "Very well, then. We'll tell it to each other."

Jamie plopped down heavily as though passing out, just at the base of the tree. She pulled her cuddly over her head and sighed. She had known it would somehow come to this: a Christmas pop-quiz, just like in school. "Is this an open-book test?" she muttered through her cuddly. Even Lindsey snickered at that one.

"Jamie, now be serious. This is important," her dad said. "A little bit of tradition won't hurt you."

"Yeah, *right*," Jamie said.

Jamie's dad opened up the family Bible to a well-worn bookmark. "Let's start here," he said, and began reading. "And there were in that same country, shepherds keeping watch over their flocks by night. And lo, the angel of the Lord came upon them; they were sore afraid. And the angel said—what, Jamie?"

"Don't be afraid, I bring good news," Jamie said.

"Fear not, for behold, I bring you good tidings of great joy," Lindsey corrected. Miss perfect show-off.

"Which is for all people," Jamie said, wrinkling her nose up into a pig-face at Lindsey.

"Which *shall be* for all people," Lindsey corrected again.

"Dad! Make her stop!" Jamie closed her eyes in frustration, and to concentrate. "For unto you today a Savior is born…" Jamie paused, and then hung her head. She was stuck. She closed her eyes again and wished she were somewhere else. But the aroma of hot spiced cider, fir needles, bayberry candles, and half-eaten candy canes didn't let her mind wander very far.

"That's okay, Kiddo. Lindsey, your turn."

"I haven't forgotten, Daddy," Lindsey said in that special pre-Christmas voice of hers that was even more sugary than Christmas fudge. The perfect little angel, at least during the Christmas shopping period. It made Jamie want to barf.

"For unto you is born this day in the city of David, a Savior, which is Christ, the Lord." Lindsey made a smirk at Jamie and then went on. "And this shall be a sign unto you; you will find the babe wrapped in swaddling clothes, lying in a manger." She beamed at her dad, and then stuck out her tongue at Jamie on the sly.

Jamie moaned and pulled her cuddly over her head again. Of course Lindsey would know it better. She'd heard it thirteen times before; Jamie had only heard it eight. Lindsey was bound to get the only lap-top this family would ever see. Jamie would only get one as an old, rusty-hinged hand-me-down. She'd probably get lots of socks and underwear instead.

She sighed and gazed through her blue cuddly at the tree lights. The star glowed bright blue, but all the smaller lights were indistinct, like green and yellow fireflies blinking off and on. She imagined each one with a doll or a toy tied to its feet, bringing them all to her.

"Okay, if that was so easy," their dad said, "Let's try another part." He flipped a bunch of pages. "Here. 'Now, when Jesus was born in Bethlehem of Judea, in the days of Herod, the king, behold, there came wise-men from the East.' Jamie, are you listening?"

Jamie uncovered her face. The fireflies were just red and yellow lights again, and the tree star was just a white plastic star with a red border, barely visible through the branches. "Yes, I'm *listening!*" Her voice sounded impatient even to *her.*

"Okay, smarty-pants," her dad said. "What did they bring?"

Jamie was silent. She pulled her cuddly over her head again to avoid looking at him. She knew he would be looking back.

"The first one brought gold," Lindsey said, still the scholar right up to the Christmas finishing flag.

"That's right," her dad said. "And his name was Baltazar. What was the second gift?"

"Frankincense!" Lindsey said. "But I don't remember his name, Daddy." Lindsey was speaking in that sickly sweet voice again, Jamie noticed. "What is Frankincense?" Lindsey added.

Her dad smiled. "It's a kind of spice people used to burn for the aroma. Like incense. It's hard to describe."

"I guess you had to *be* there," Jamie muttered absently, looking at all the lights. Her dad had strung a strand of lights over the mantle again. The lights dangled above the nativity scene there, spinning just enough to twinkle. Jamie could just see the upper halves of Mary and Joseph from where she lay. They looked like two sticks of cinnamon, and the manger looked like a piece of chocolate. Just for a moment, she wondered what it must have been like to hunker down in a stable and have a baby. Probably cold, and entirely without chocolate.

Her dad sipped his cider and then continued. "And tradition has it that his name was Melchior. Good, Lindsey. Now let Jamie answer."

"Dad," Jamie whined. "Do we have to know their names?"

"It's part of the Christmas story," he answered. "It's one of the greatest stories of all time, and I think you should learn it. Now, who was the third wise man, and what did he bring?"

"Santa Claus," Jamie muttered. "And he brought toys." She rolled onto her side facing away from them and looked at all the pretty boxes under the tree. She already knew which ones were for her. Well, if she didn't get her lap-top, at least she could hope for something from Santa good enough to tell the kids about at school.

Jamie's dad sighed.

"His name was Casper, stupid!" Lindsey said.

"Like in Casper the Friendly Ghost?" Jamie made a wan smile, hoping her joke would lighten things up. It didn't.

"Gaspar, with a G," her dad corrected.

"Whatever," Lindsey said. "But he brought myrrh, I know."

"*Duh*," Jamie said.

"Oh, you didn't know *any* of it, Dork-meister!" Lindsey glowered at her.

"Did so!" Jamie said. "Anyway, knowing this stuff is important *how*?"

"Every single piece of knowledge is valuable," her dad shrugged. "Who knows, maybe you'll be on *Jeopardy* one day, and the category will be Christmas. Now, settle down."

"Like, if I name the three wise men, do I win a lap-top?" Jamie glowered back at Lindsey, who gasped in dismay.

"At least I'm the *smart* one," Lindsey said. "I could really use a lap-top."

"Yeah, for storing boys' phone numbers," Jamie said.

"Would not! I'd do my homework on it. School's very important to me." Lindsey held her hand to her chest, the perfect princess.

"Is that why you wear a Victoria's Secret bra to school?" Jamie said.

"You little dork!" Lindsey shouted and threw a pillow at her. Jamie ducked, and the pillow hit the tree, knocking several of the glass angels to the floor.

"Girls! Enough! Now look what you've done!" Their dad rushed to the tree and started picking up the angels, examining each one for damage.

"I didn't mean to," Lindsey said.

"It happened on accident," Jamie said.

"Yeah, on accident," Lindsey echoed.

"Nothing broken. No harm done." Their father sounded tired. He closed the book and pulled out all the bookmarks. "But I suppose that's as far as we're going to get with our reading this year. It's time for bed, both of you."

"But you said we could open presents!" Jamie said, her hands on her hips.

"Yeah, Dad, you *promised!*" Lindsey chimed in, for once on Jamie's side.

"I said I'd think about it," he answered.

"*Dad!*" This time the girls were in perfect unison.

"Okay, okay," their dad grinned. "I'd better keep my promises." He reached behind the tree. "But just one each. And I get to choose which one. Lindsey, this is for you." He handed her a small flat present.

Lindsey opened it in record time. It was a CD. But her gleeful look faded rapidly. "*Christmas* music?" Lindsey sounded as if this were a most unbelievable catastrophe.

"I thought you liked that group," her dad said.

"I like their *real* music," Lindsey said under her breath.

"Well, try it anyway. Who knows, you might even like it…*on accident*," he said, mimicking the two of them.

Lindsey placed the disc in her player and put on her earphones. After a moment, her eyebrows went up and her frown disappeared, although Jamie could tell she was determined *not* to smile.

"Okay?" her dad asked.

"Tolerable," Lindsey shrugged. "I get the bathroom first!" she added, waltzing away toward the bathroom without so much as a backward glance.

"You're welcome," her dad said after her. "And merry Christmas Eve, Lindsey."

"Oh yeah, thanks, Dad." Lindsey's voice came from the bathroom just as the door clicked shut.

"What about me, me, *me*?" Jamie said.

"I was just getting to you." He reached behind the tree again and brought out an odd-looking package. It was shaped like a fat pop bottle and gathered into a bow at the top. Jamie hadn't seen that one before.

When she opened it, she stared in amazement and then frowned. It was a wooden statue, about as tall as the span of her open hand, of the most peculiar looking angel Jamie had ever seen. He was old and pot-bellied, bald and wrinkled. His wings were tattered, with feathers askew or missing entirely.

He needed a shave, and his halo had slipped down over one ear. He had a bent and battered trumpet tied to a sash around his waist. His smile was not very heavenly, either. It was more like the smile of someone who had gotten into the Christmas cookies. "What is *this*?" Jamie stared at her strange present.

"That's the Christmas angel, Jamie," her dad answered.

"Christmas angel? But it's so, so…*ugly!*" Jamie stamped her foot, mostly out of frustration over not getting to choose which present to open.

Her dad paused to take a sip from his mug, and then exhaled noisily. "*Ahh*. Hmm. Well, it's true he won't be winning any beauty contests. But, well, there's just something a little magic about him. One day you'll understand. You'll have to trust me on this one, Kiddo."

Jamie examined the old tattered angel top to bottom, front and back. No lights, no sounds, no battery compartment. Not much magic here. "Sure," she muttered, and dropped the Christmas angel onto the couch.

The bathroom door was still closed; Jamie turned back to her dad. "Dad, can I have my three questions now?" When her father tucked her into bed, he nearly always told her she could ask three questions. Then he would be honor-bound to answer them truthfully.

"Hmm, seeing as how Lindsey has the bathroom all tied up, okay, shoot. If they're quick."

Jamie thought hard, her mouth tightening into a small crooked line. She twiddled with her ponytail over her shoulder. It smelled like fir needles and bayberry candles, with a touch of peppermint. She nibbled on the end of it. "First question," she said. "Dad, what was your most favoritest gift that Santa ever gave you?"

Her dad smiled a slight parent kind of smile, the kind that no kid ever understood. "My most favorite gift didn't come from Santa, Jamie. Santa just brings toys after Christmas is over. The best gifts are gifts of love, and they're usually given on Christmas Eve." He gave Jamie a little hug. "Like this one. Merry Christmas Eve, Kiddo."

"What time do you think Santa will get here?" Jamie asked.

"Long after you're asleep. And that was your second question."

"I didn't say second question!" Jamie stamped her foot again.

Lindsey leaned into the room and yelled out, "Bathroom's free," and disappeared again.

"Well, you have one more, Kiddo, so make it a good one," her dad said. Jamie looked around the room, trying to think of a good question. It was impossible for her to remain unhappy or even very disappointed amid all the decorations. She truly enjoyed the season's preparations—taping Christmas cards in the hallway, frosting the windows, putting the star on top of the tree, setting up the nativity scene in its special place on the mantle above the fireplace. But her dad was so picky about where the figurines went that most of the time, she and Lindsey just backed away and let him do it. Jamie would watch him standing by the mantle, sipping his cider and fiddling with the angels and the wise men. He would pick them up one by one, examine them for chips and cracks, (someone had dropped one of the sheep once and broken off a leg) and then he would set them down just so in various spots around the nativity scene.

Over the top, Jamie thought. Who cared about the names of the wise men, or how many angels went where? She sighed, but the fir and bayberry scents calmed her and made her smile a little.

"Okay, third question." Jamie paused and took a quick nibble on the end of her pony-tail again. "Dad, how come you're so picky about the manger scene? Do you believe all that stuff in the Christmas story?"

Her dad smiled that unreadable smile again. "I believe it…" He paused, thinking. "just as much as if I'd seen it. But everyone has to come to their own conclusions, I think. Now, go on, Jamie. Lindsey's out of the bathroom."

Jamie took one more look around the living room, her eyes settling on the mantle-top nativity scene and the large glass angel her dad had placed beside the manger. He had tapped a few suspended lights so that they swayed; the angel beside the manger seemed to twinkle under them. "I wonder what really *did* happen way back then," she said to herself. "I wish I could just go and see for myself. And not the cardboard stand-up version, either. I mean the real thing—camel breath, donkey poop, and all. That's the only way I could ever believe it."

"Well, it's a wonderful story whether you believe any of it or not," her dad said. "Now, off to bed with you."

"Will you come and tuck me in?"

"Yes, in a few minutes," he answered. He picked up the Christmas angel from the couch and gazed at it for a moment, turning it slowly in his hand.

Jamie scampered off toward the bathroom.

"Had the little statue actually moved?"

CHAPTER 2

GABE

After Jamie had climbed into bed, just as her feet were starting to warm up wrapped inside her cuddly, her dad lumbered in and sat on the edge of her bed. He tousled her hair lightly—more like straightening than a tousling, really. He smiled and kissed her cheek. "Merry Christmas Eve," he said. "Your mom called. She said to say she's sorry she has to work on Christmas Eve, but she'll be here first thing in the morning."

Jamie's mom's job was to be the first nurse to see people who came in the Emergency Room doors. Christmas to Jamie's mom was a wonderful time, too. But it was also a busy time for the hospital, and she had been unable to get Christmas Eve off. She had said she would make it up to the girls. That could mean extra presents. Between Mom and Santa, all hopes for a good Christmas haul were not lost.

"Will she be here when I wake up?"

"I'm sure she will," her dad answered.

"Good. I'll probably want to open presents right away." Jamie liked to plan ahead. Especially ahead to Christmas morning.

"Try not to get too far ahead of yourself, Kiddo," her dad said. "Sleep first."

"I'm not going to sleep tonight. I'm going to stay awake and listen for Santa."

Jamie's dad tucked her in anyway. "Suit yourself," he said. "But no one ever sees him. They say that sometimes you can hear his reindeer on the rooftop, though."

"Dad, did you ever hear Santa Claus when you were a kid?"

"No. Now, no more questions. Try to sleep." He started to rise, but her hand stopped him.

"Dad, you never really answered my first question tonight," Jamie said. "What was the most favoritest gift you ever got?"

Her dad looked down at her and smiled. "I've had so many wonderful gifts. I have my job, my health, a wonderful family..."

"Not that kind of stuff," Jamie said. "I mean an actual gift from somebody on Christmas."

"Well then," he said, "I guess it would have to be this." He pulled the Christmas angel from his pocket and set it on Jamie's night-stand. The angel's rough edges glowed dimly in the light from Jamie's night light. "I found it at the very bottom of the Christmas chest in the attic this year. I'd forgotten all about it. My father gave it to me when I was about your age. Lindsey's too old to appreciate it, so I'm giving it to you."

"*That's* your best gift? No train sets, or remote controlled sports cars? No big TVs? That's *dumb*!" Jamie's hopes for a good haul were definitely sliding downhill. This was probably going to be a socks and underwear kind of Christmas. Maybe Santa would bring something. She'd stay awake and listen.

"Well, you asked, and I told you. Actually, I thought it was a dumb gift too, at first. But I learned that it was given with a great deal of love, and I don't doubt it carries much love with it even yet. Now, good night and sweet dreams. I love you, Jamie."

"Night, Dad. Love you too," Jamie said just as the door closed.

A line of light shone from underneath the door. She watched it until, after a few moments, it went out too. She listened for sounds like sleigh bells or hooves on roof shingles, but she only heard a few of the normal evening bumps, and occasionally a quiet voice. In the dim glow of her night light, she could just barely see across her room to where her dolls and teddy bears sat along the wall. She only had two Barbies, but she had more teddy bears than anyone she knew. She had won them from the grabber machine in the supermarket entrance. She tried to remember their names, just to stay awake.

"Let's see, there's Lily-Bear, and Lumpy-Bear, there's Sailor-Bear, and Yum-yum…"

"Jamie"

Jamie rubbed her eyes and poked at her ears. She must have nodded off for a second; she had thought she heard someone say her name. Well, she was all that more determined to stay awake. "Let's see, where was I? Oh yes, Yum-yum. And that's Jessie-Bear, and Erin-Bear..."

"Jamie"

The voice was louder this time, and she was definitely not asleep. But there was no one there. At least, no one that she could see. She scooted down under the covers and drew her cuddly up from her toes all in one motion. With her cuddly over her head like a jacket hood, she peered around the room.

"Jamie!"

This time she heard it unmistakably. It had come from the direction of her night-stand. She looked at the Christmas angel. Had it changed position?

Suddenly, the Christmas angel began to glow in a soft, pale light, like moonlight, in which everything appeared to be the same color. And it began to move as well. It flapped one wing as if testing it, and then extended the other wing in a long, slow stretch. Feathers pointed every which-way, like quills on a half-bald porcupine. The angel was definitely peering back at her. Jamie went all the way under the covers and pulled her cuddly in after her like a cork.

After awhile, she peeked out with one eye. The angel was sitting on the edge of her night-stand with his head cocked way over to one side, as though looking for something under a table.

"Don't be afraid," the Christmas angel said. They stared at each other awhile longer before the angel spoke again. "Come out, come out, wherever you are!" he said in a sing-song voice. Jamie shook her head. "Ollie, ollie, ox-in-free?" the angel chanted, ending in an upward sound, like a question.

"I don't think so," Jamie said.

"Ready or not, here I come?" The angel was resting his chin in his hand and tapping his cheek with one finger.

"Don't you dare!" Jamie said.

"Look, kid, come on out of there and we can have a chat." The angel motioned with his hand.

"Nuh-uh, I don't think so!" Jamie said, her voice quivering just a little bit.

They stared at each other awhile longer before the angel spoke again.

"I'm a nice guy, really. Wouldn't hurt a fly. Actually, I have trouble catching them anymore." He flapped his wings, and one of his feathers kept on swinging like a pendulum after he stopped. He tucked it back into place. "Can't you come out just a little-ity-bit?" The angel held up a finger and thumb, close together.

"I'm not supposed to talk to strangers," Jamie said.

"*Hmmm.* That's pretty good advice." The angel stroked his scraggly stubble of a beard. "But Jamie, didn't your father give me to you? I'm yours now. Don't you ever talk to your dolls?"

"Maybe sometimes," Jamie answered, poking her head out just a little, holding her cuddly out in front of her like a shield. "But they never *ever* talk back. How did you know my name, anyway?"

"I'm an angel," the angel said, lifting his chin up and spreading his wings out wide, flapping them slowly. He glowed a little brighter, too, but lost a couple of wing feathers in the flourish. He scooped them up and tried to poke them back into place. "Got any duct tape?" he asked.

Jamie giggled in spite of herself. "Who are you?" she asked.

"Oh my goodness," the angel gasped. "Where are my manners? I forgot to introduce myself, didn't I? Time was, everybody knew *me*. Now, well, *ahem*." He straightened his pale ankle-length robe, slicked back his sparse hair, and tucked in his wings as best he could. "My name is Gabriel, but my friends call me Gabe. Pleased to meet you." He reached out his hand to shake, but Jamie shied away from it. He withdrew his hand and straightened a stray lock of hair, pretending that that was what he had intended to do all along. "I need a shave and a haircut, don't I? Christmas sort of snuck up on me this year. Listen, I know I'm—what did you say—'so, so, *ugly!*'" he said in a voice just like she had said it earlier. "But listen. I'm not really ugly; I'm just starting to moult, and it's not a pretty sight at my age. In my day, though, I used to turn some heads, let me tell you."

"How old are you?" Jamie asked.

Gabriel glanced at his wrist where a tiny hourglass was held in place with duct tape. "Four thousand, five hundred and seventy-ish. Give or take a decade," he answered.

"So wait," Jamie said. "Your name is *Gabriel?*"

"You can call me Gabe," the angel said.

"So my dad reads the Bible to us sometimes. I remember one of the archangels is named Gabriel."

"That's me," Gabriel said.

"You're *the* Gabriel, as in, the Archangel Gabriel blew his horn, and the heavens opened up?" Jamie said.

Gabriel nodded. "Retired," he shrugged. His wings moved when he did. "Michael's got the job now. Big Mike. Has the most humongous wings you ever did see. Oh, sure, he can blow his horn louder than anyone now. But he only knows, like, three notes. Me, I've been practicing." Gabriel grinned and untied a tiny horn from the side of his belt. It was a silver trumpet, with the bell bent upwards at a 45 degree angle. He winked and played a riff of an old Dizzy Gillespie tune. "Got a new teacher," he said.

"What are you doing here?" Jamie said.

"It's Christmas Eve, don't you know. It's a time for giving gifts, and I have a gift for *you*, Jamie."

"You do?"

"I heard your Christmas wish, and I've come to grant it," Gabriel said.

"You're giving me a lap-top computer?" Jamie sat up in bed.

"I think it was that *other* wish. Don't you remember?"

Jamie frowned. "You're not a socks and underwear kind of angel, are you?"

Gabriel thought about that for a moment. "Jamie, what if socks and underwear were what you needed most in the whole universe? What if you were so cold and hungry you'd be thankful for a few rags and bread crumbs?"

Jamie laughed a short little laugh, more like a snort. "Hah! I can't imagine that!"

Gabriel smiled widely, showing uneven teeth. "That's why I'm here."

"You're here to give me socks and underwear?"

"No." Gabriel said. "I'm here to give you what you most need in the whole universe."

"What's that?" Jamie brightened.

"Perspective," Gabriel muttered very quietly.

"What did you say? Is it battery operated?" Jamie asked.

Gabriel shook his head. "Maybe I'd better explain. You see, Jamie, Christmas Eve is a very special celebration. Almost the first thing a lot of new angels want to do, after meeting all their friends and relatives and such, is they want to know what really happened on that first Christmas Eve way back in Bethlehem. But in heaven, time sort of goes any which way you want it to. So in heaven, every day is Christmas Eve. Angels get to fly back to Bethlehem all the time. Did you ever read that part of Luke where it says, 'suddenly a multitude of angels appeared'?"

"We didn't get that far this year," Jamie said. "But we did last year. I liked that part, too, about the singing." Jamie sighed.

"Ah, child, you should hear such singing." Gabriel smiled and shook his head. "Even Luke didn't believe there were so many. A multitude—hah! There were millions!"

"So, you're saying the Christmas story really *happened?*" Jamie said.

"It's still happening, Kiddo," Gabriel said. "I'm the Christmas angel now. I'm still working on it. I take new arrivals back to that first Christmas night in Bethlehem. I used to take four or five at a time, but I'm not as young as I used to be. Besides, they kept me awfully busy, and I never got to see any of my friends. Anyway, angels aren't as much fun as real people."

"But what does any of that have to do with me?" Jamie asked.

"You made the wish. You said you wished you could go see what really happened back in Bethlehem on Christmas night. People wonder about that this time of year. So, once every Christmas Eve, your Christmas Eve that is, I can take one new angel back to Bethlehem for an eye-witness view. Interested?"

"But I'm not an angel. I'm just a girl."

"Yes, I know, I know, and you won't be a real *real* angel for, let's see," Gabriel glanced at his hourglass.

"Well, never mind. Long time. But Jamie, all you have to do is make that particular wish on Christmas Eve, and the part of you that wishes becomes an angel the whole rest of the night. Provided, of course, that you take my hand." Gabriel grinned, rubbed his hands together, and held one out.

"I don't know about this," Jamie said.

"Come on, Jamie. Think of it as an adventure! You can even think of it as a dream if you like, but it's more than that. Come on, take my hand. I heard you wish it already. Didn't you say that seeing is believing? Don't be afraid. You'll love the ride. Piece of cake!" Gabriel slowly extended his hand closer. "All you have to do is take my hand and say the words."

Jamie slowly reached out and tried to grasp the angel's hand, but she couldn't feel it at all. In fact, her hand passed right through Gabriel's hand, but she held it there anyway. "What do I say?" she said.

"What have we been *talking* about, Kiddo? *Hello?*" Gabriel sighed. "Sorry. I've been a little tense lately. It's part of my PMS– um, my Pre-Moulting Syndrome. But I can't say the wish for you, don't you know. It has to come from your heart alone," Gabriel said.

"I still don't know about this," Jamie said.

"Well, make up your mind," Gabriel said, glancing at his hourglass. "I still have time to talk your sister into going."

The thought of Lindsey getting to do something that *she* didn't get to do was what finally made Jamie's mind up for her. "Wait!" She said. "I want to go. I do."

"Say it then."

Jamie took a deep breath and closed her eyes to concentrate. "I wish I could go back to Bethlehem on that first Christmas night," she said.

When Jamie opened her eyes, she noticed that Gabriel was getting larger. The old angel kept on growing until he was just two fingers taller than Jamie, and then reached out his hand toward her. When she slowly grasped it, the hand was there this time. She could feel the infinite strength yet gentleness in it. Then she began to feel a warm, wonderful feeling that flowed to every part of her, and she began to glow in a pale, colorless light, just like Gabriel.

Gabriel laughed and jumped up and down, his stomach half a bounce behind the rest of him. "That's the spirit! Hang on now. You mustn't let go, Jamie."

"Or what?" Jamie said.

"The angel light starts to dim."

"What then?" Jamie asked.

"Well, after awhile, you'd be a little girl again. But don't worry about it." Gabriel smiled and untied his battered trumpet from his belt. "I've never misplaced a single soul." He started to put the trumpet to his lips, and paused. "At least not yet," he said, and shrugged. His wings flapped as he did so.

Then he put the trumpet to his lips, and played a lively riff. Swirls of light leapt from the bell of the trumpet and settled down onto the bed in the shape of an old stone wishing well. "You've made the Christmas wish, child. Let's go make it come true. Hang on tight!" Gabriel tried to jump up and flap his wings, but the feathers were so irregular that some of them interlaced like fingers. He fell down.

"D-word," he said, pulling them apart with his free hand. Then he jumped again, this time taking flight and pulling Jamie along after him with a snap.

"What do you mean, at least not ye—?" Jamie was saying, just as Gabriel flew head-first into the well and pulled her in after him. The last thing she saw was an extremely bright light at the bottom of the well.

"You did make a wish, didn't you?"

CHAPTER 3

ANY-WHEN

Jamie felt as though she were floating downward, almost weightless, with a gentle breeze blowing through her nightgown. She held on tightly to Gabriel with one hand and onto her cuddly with the other. She could see Gabriel clearly in the pale light coming from them both as the old angel huffed and wheezed his way into the darkness. Behind her, the top of the well receded like a point of light getting smaller and smaller.

Suddenly, white lights appeared like bubbles all around her. They were moving, coming closer. And as they neared, Jamie could see shapes within them. Wings.

Soon Gabriel and Jamie were surrounded by countless white lights coming from as far away in any direction as anyone cared to look. And from inside the lights, excited, gleeful faces looked out. Some were young, some were old; some were fat, and some were thin. Some were boys and some were girls. Some had wings, and some had just a feather or two. Some, like Jamie, had no wings at all. But all of them seemed happy and were grinning so wide that Jamie could not help but feel quite a bit less frightened.

"Where are we, Gabriel?" Jamie said. "Is this heaven?"

"No, Jamie. Heaven's a lot nicer. This is, well, this is in-between. Usually, souls pass through here so fast, they don't see much. Most people think it's some sort of tunnel. But it's really big and wide, and lots of fun, too. You'll see." Gabriel shook his head. "Everybody's in such a hurry to arrive, they miss the journey itself."

Just then the circles of light reached them. Hundreds of angels floated up to Gabriel and swirled around him like dolphins around a toy ball, spinning him in their wake.

"Careful! Careful!" Gabriel kept repeating, along with, "Glad to see you!"

Many voices came to Jamie, all as joyful as could be. A few of them seemed familiar. One voice stood out in particular. She turned around to see a red-haired angel with big lips.

"Ohh, I've heard about Jerusalem!" the red-haired angel said. "Honey, could we stop there and go to the bazaar?"

"Well, I'll try to arrange it for you, baby," said an Hispanic man with slicked back hair as he lit up a cigar. "Hey, you with the trumpet," he said toward Gabriel. "You play?"

Gabriel chuckled, more of a snort, really. "Do I play the trumpet?" He pried the old bent trumpet from his sash. "You're asking Gabriel if he plays the horn?" He played a fast riff that seemed to contain within it all of the Christmas songs Jamie had ever heard. She laughed and clapped her hands.

"Say, you're pretty good. Have a cigar," the man said.

"No thanks. I'm trying to quit," Gabriel said.

"Say, I'm getting some people together for a band. We could do a gig in Bethlehem."

"I've made other arrangements," Gabriel said. "But we can always use more musicians. Why don't *you* join *us*?"

"I'll talk to my boys," the man said. "Say, could we stop at the bazaar? I told my wife—"

"Sorry, no unscheduled stops," Gabriel said. "I believe this is an express flight."

"Ay, carumba!" the man said. "What'll I tell her?"

"Tell her to decide what's important, or she'll lose her way," Gabriel answered.

The Hispanic man sighed. "Sure you won't have a cigar?" he said. "They're Cuban."

"Really?" Gabe smacked his lips. "Cuban, ay?" But just as he was taking the cigar, an old wrinkled face popped in between them. It belonged to a short, clean-shaven, elderly man wearing glasses with the thickest lenses Jamie had ever seen.

"Age before beauty," the elderly man said as he snatched the cigar from Gabriel's hand.

"Well, help yourself," Gabriel said, "But I'm older."

"I made it past a hundred," the elderly man said, straightening up with pride.

Gabriel pointed at himself with his thumb. "Four thousand, five hundred seventy," he said.

"-ish," Jamie added. Gabriel frowned at her.

The elderly man looked the old angel up and down. "Hmm," he said. "Should have said beauty before age. Might have had a chance then."

Gabriel took back the cigar, lit it off a nearby halo, and coughed several times. "These are good," he said, gasping for air.

"Over here! Maybe someone will know the way!" a thin old angel in a white nun's habit said as she pulled along another, a slender, blonde-haired angel. They hustled up to within an arm's length of Jamie. "Please, can anyone help us? We're on our way to Bethlehem," the old nun added.

"Us, too!" Jamie said.

"Oh! Do you know the way? I do *so* want to see the baby Jesus!" the old nun said.

"No," Jamie said. "But Gabriel does."

"The way to Bethlehem is illuminated by desire," Gabriel said. "And your desire is so heart-felt, it is blazing a trail for us all."

Just then, an extremely loud double trumpet blast nearly knocked everyone off their feet. It certainly would have, Jamie thought, had anybody been standing on anything. She clung to Gabriel's hand like a vise. Several of the smaller angels began to whimper. The younger angel with the blonde hair hid behind the old nun.

"There, there, nothing to be afraid of," the old nun said, stroking the blonde head behind her.

"Absolutely not, princess," the elderly man with the thick glasses said. "Most all the *papparazzi* go the other way." He held out a hand, thumb downward.

The old nun gave him a stern but tolerant look before she continued. "What I meant was that no one need have anything to fear once this babe is born," she said.

"Amen to that, sister," Gabriel said. "*Except me that is, if I'm late,*" he muttered under his breath, but Jamie was close enough to hear.

Off in the distance, Jamie could see a glow. A bright light began to shine downwards, away from what looked like the horizon. Its light flowed toward them like a gentle stream. Then a glowing ball appeared above the horizon and began to move down the stream in rhythmic jerks. The glow became a line of glows, and then two lines of glows, each one sprouting an enormous pair of wings. And at the very front of the two lines marched the largest, handsomest, proudest angel of them all. His wings were so large that the angels on either side of him had to help hold them up. The proud angel carried a long, single-chambered horn that was as tall as he was. He and his wing bearers marched right up to Gabriel's gathering just as the golden river of light reached them. The proud angel's wing bearers knocked several of the tinier angels in their path a-tumbling.

Gabriel, the old nun, and the blonde-haired princess gathered the smallest angels in their arms and set them upright again, smoothing the feathers of those that had wings, and calming the ones who were bleating like lost sheep. "There now, *shh*, it'll be alright," Gabriel said again and again.

Jamie heard the blonde angel say, "So many are alone! How can we help them all?"

"Just do the work that is before you," the old nun said as she picked up another wingless child. "*Shh*," she added, stroking the little one's hair. "You don't have to be alone any more."

When they all finally stood up, Jamie heard popping sounds, and two huge feathers appeared on the old nun's and the blonde haired angel's backs. As the two of them gasped and beamed at each other, another smaller feather popped out of Gabriel's left ear. Gabriel frowned with embarrassment, plucked the feather from his ear and threw it away.

"I used to have wings like Michael's," Gabriel pointed at the proud angel as he whispered to Jamie. "But feathers are kind of like hair. You reach an age when you never know *where* they're going to grow."

"They just pop out of nowhere?" Jamie asked.

"No, no," Gabriel said. "Angels get their wings by caring for others. Every time they do an act of kindness for another, they get a feather. Sometimes two, if they help a great deal. Course, if they act mean, they lose them even faster. All at once if they're really bad. We call it moulting, but that's just a nice word for a funk. The idea is to help one another so that we don't get so lonely."

"How come Michael doesn't lose feathers? He doesn't seem very nice."

"Oh, he really is, deep inside. He's just a little puffed up with himself lately. Besides, archangels don't lose their feathers. They have enough to worry about without that."

"Hey, I thought that it was supposed to be that when bells rang, angels got their wings," Jamie said.

"Bells?" Gabriel stroked his beard. "Bells are nice. God likes bells. But I don't think—where'd you read that, in the *Enquirer*?"

Just then, a deep voice boomed out. **"The procession is about to begin!"**

Michael raised the massive horn to his lips. Almost all the angels in Gabriel's group quickly held their hands over their ears. Some of the tiniest ones began to whimper again.

"Michael, Michael," Gabriel held his wing-tip over the bell of Michael's horn. "Chill out. We have little ones present."

Michael appeared annoyed momentarily, but then smiled, a cat-hunting-a-bird kind of smile. "Well, Gabriel, I see you're making the trip one more *time!*" Michael punctuated the word *time* by giving Gabriel a hearty slap on the back.

Gabriel spun all the way around with the force of the blow, breaking a feather and pulling Jamie into the spiral after him.

"Sure you can keep up, old man?" Michael added.

Gabriel examined his broken feather. "Easy come, easy go," he sighed. "No problem, Mike," Gabriel grinned. "I'll manage just dandy. Hope you get a couple of feathers for your concern. But how about you let me play the marching song, big guy?" Cheers rang out from everywhere.

Michael looked around. He would have frowned if he hadn't been an archangel. Instead, he smiled that cat-like smile again, and held out his hand, palm up, toward Gabriel.

Gabriel swung Jamie onto his back, between his wings. "Hold on tight, Kiddo. We're about to start the biggest Christmas parade you'll ever see!" He untied the little trumpet from his sash and raised it to his lips. "Just say the word, Mike."

"I wish you'd call the archangel of the Lord **Michael!**" Thunder and lightning occurred in the distance as Michael spoke.

Gabriel bowed ever so slightly. "I meant to say Michael, your holy horn-ship," Gabriel coughed, cleared his throat, and whispered over his shoulder to Jamie. "Three thousand years ago, I would have tied his wing feathers together and called him Mikey. As a matter of fact, I seem to recall that I did," Gabriel chuckled at the thought.

"**Is everybody ready?**" Michael voice boomed out. Voices cheered from everywhere; circles of light were still coming toward them from as far away as Jamie could see.

"Big angels hold hands with the little ones!" the old nun whispered loudly, taking hold of two tiny angels beside her. Several angels near her did the same.

"A wonderful idea, sister," Gabriel said. "As much as the two of you have shown your love for children, perhaps you wouldn't mind helping me look after them. Some of them come here all alone without anyone to greet them, don't you know." Gabriel stroked his scraggly beard. "*Hmm*. In fact, it's such a good idea—" He took a deep breath and said in a loud voice for all to hear: **"Big ones hold hands with the little ones!"**

"*Ahem!*" Michael said, looking at Gabriel with hard eyes. "I believe I'm in charge here now."

"Sorry. Habit," Gabriel grinned.

"But these two *do* seem well suited for that job. Besides, you've already got a job." Michael looked down his nose at the old nun, and then said in a kinder voice, "I think the two of you will do nicely as guardians of the littlest new arrivals." Cheers rose up from all the angels nearby.

"Now, what was I going to say?" Michael frowned and put a finger to his lips, then held it up in the air. "Oh, yes. *Ahem*. **Big ones hold the hands of the little ones!**" The archangel said, although Jamie thought he'd said it with a little less concern than the old nun. Everybody cheered again anyway, eager to go.

Michael raised his humongous horn, and all the angels close to him scattered, their hands held tightly over their ears. He sighed and gestured to Gabriel. An actual smile appeared on his face. "You're pretty good on that little trumpet, but I have to open the gate."

"Thank you, Michael." Gabriel pumped the trumpet valves to warm them up. "Cover your ears, everybody!" Gabriel said to all those nearby.

"Let the procession begin!" Michael said in a voice that could be heard everywhere at once. His horn blast would have shaken the ground, had there been any, and a flurry of tiny wisps of twinkling light emerged from the bell of his horn. The lights stretched out before him all the way to the horizon and became a path. At the end of the path, on the edge of the horizon, a star appeared. Michael began to march along the path, followed by his wing bearers. And trailing after, more circles of light than Jamie could possibly have a number for.

Gabriel stroked his beard and said, "Hmm, well, let me see now." He raised his trumpet and began to play. The music that came out seemed to contain within it many songs at once, some that Jamie recognized, and many that she did not. Gabriel paused after a long flurry of notes to catch his breath. **"Join in!"** he said, in a voice that all could hear. **"Sing in your own way the joy that you feel in your heart!"** he shouted. Then he began to play again.

Voices joined in immediately. Each angel seemed to hear the accompaniment to their own song. Many songs, all different, yet all with the same underlying marching cadence. Countless voices, one rhythmic outpouring of joy. They echoed from every direction and filled Jamie's ears entirely, until her own voice sprang forth almost involuntarily. She heard herself singing *Adeste Fidelis*, and Gabe's trumpet seemed to be keeping perfect time with only her song; her eyes got a little moist with joy. She looked around and noticed that the eyes of all the angels nearby were moist, no matter what they were singing. Gabriel winked at her and smiled. He winked at several others, too, and then began marching; his wings moved gently to help him along his way. From her vantage point on Gabriel's back, Jamie could see all the little balls of light pointing like a wedge toward Michael, who marched steadily toward the star. Behind her, there was no end of the line anywhere.

Gabriel's wings flapped back and forth in their own odd way as Jamie held on tightly to where they attached to his shoulders. Soon Gabriel was huffing and wheezing; he had to put down his trumpet to catch his breath, but the music continued unabated. Several of the younger angels passed him up. It was apparent to Jamie that the new star was their destination, but before it had gotten much bigger at all, Gabriel's wings slowed and drooped.

"I'm pooped," he wheezed. "Let's camp here." Gabriel sat down as though he were sitting in an imaginary chair, and a chair appeared just as he did so. Jamie barely had enough time to slide off his back and take his hand again.

"Won't we be late?" she said.

"Nah," Gabriel answered, still out of breath. "We just won't be early. Anyways, I've seen it a thousand times."

"Well, I haven't!" Jamie said. "Come on, I'll carry you." Jamie put one of Gabriel's wings over her shoulder and struggled upwards. At first, neither of them moved. Then, slowly, both of them began to rise and move forward toward the star. But it wasn't Jamie who was doing the carrying. Several young, strong angels had appeared beneath them and were carrying them both along.

"Let us carry *you* now, Gabriel," one of them said.

"As you carried *us* so many years ago," another said.

"And we'll carry your friend, too," still another said from underneath Jamie.

Just then a pale, slender angel with long black hair passed along side of them; he was walking backward, but looked like he was walking forward. An angel who was struggling to walk backward while holding onto the front of Gabriel's chair said to him, "Hey, you're pretty good at that! Can you give us a hand?" The pale angel gave a beautiful smile. He spun around twice, then danced in perfect cadence to the music around them, and grabbed onto Gabriel's chair with one gloved hand.

"Bless you! Bless you all!" Gabriel said. Feathers sprouted everywhere. Two shot right past Jamie's face so close that she had to move them aside to speak to Gabriel.

"What is *that*?" Jamie said, pointing to the star, which was now so close that she could see it had a hole in the middle, like a huge, glowing doughnut. Up ahead, the archangel Michael had almost reached it already.

"That's the gateway of all our hopes and desires," Gabriel said. "I just call it Any-when."

"I don't understand," Jamie said.

"Well, time and distance are not the same here, Jamie. We can go anywhere and any-when we wish. We travel by desire. Do you remember when you made your Christmas wish, and the wishing well appeared?"

"Yes," Jamie said.

"Well then, there you have it," Gabriel said.

"Have what?" Jamie said.

"*Voila*," Gabriel pointed. "The Christmas star."

"Whoa," Jamie gasped. "You mean *the* Christmas star, like, over Bethlehem? You mean it wasn't a real star?"

"Isn't, Jamie. Isn't a real star," Gabriel corrected her. "In heaven, everything is present tense because everything is happening right now. No, Jamie, what people call the Christmas star is just Any-when, and thousands and thousands of angels streaming down through it to see a special little baby. But it won't be over Bethlehem. At least not yet."

"Why not?"

"Nobody can arrive until after the baby is born. It's a matter of privacy, don't you know. Mary wants it that way." Gabriel chuckled. "It's kind of a celestial joke. All the eager ones go through Any-when first, and then they have to hang around for weeks just circling and circling. Us more experienced types like to hang back a bit. It's all in the timing. Trust me on this one, Kiddo." Gabriel produced his new cigar from behind his ear and lit it off a nearby halo.

Michael arrived at the glowing ring. "Here we are! Any-when!" he boomed out. "Four abreast, no crowding! Step right up, best seats in front. A few more altos on this side. Tenors, let's go, let's go!" he said repeatedly.

As Gabriel and Jamie drew nearer, Jamie could see that the star with the hole in it had changed. It now looked like a huge golden gate with double swinging doors. It looked rather like pictures Jamie had seen of what people thought heaven's front doors would look like.

As the two of them arrived at the gate on the shoulders of the other angels, Michael took down his horn and placed it across the gateway, blocking their way.

"Well, well," Michael said. "Tuckered already, Gabriel? Maybe you should stay behind."

"I'll be fine, thanks for caring," Gabriel said. "May you receive a thousand feathers, great one."

"Don't need them." Michael grinned, stretching out one wing to admire it. Then he gave Gabriel a rough hug.

"Is Any-when heaven's gate, too?" Jamie asked. She tried to look through but couldn't see a thing.

"No, child," Michael said, his voice a bit gentler with her. "Heaven's gate is over that way. But heaven's gate is just a focus point like this one, only bigger."

"This is a what?" Jamie asked.

"It's millions of souls all wishing the same thing, just as you must have, child. You did make a wish, didn't you?" Michael looked stern again.

"Yes, sir," Jamie answered, not at all sure that was such a good thing.

"And I just came to get her piece of it," Gabriel said excitedly.

"My piece of *what?*" Jamie was thoroughly confused, but there was no stopping Gabriel for an explanation.

"And the best part is," Gabriel chortled, "I never know what that piece will be!"

"Well, take good care of her, old man. No slip ups. Have a nice trip." Michael turned quickly back toward the line of angels, which was bunching up. "Here now, only four at a time! Heads-of-State, quit crowding, I say!"

"Gabriel," Jamie whispered, "What do you mean you don't—"

Just then, as Michael stretched out his arms to direct the others, one of his magnificent wings bumped Gabriel squarely in the back.

"know—" Jamie was saying just as Gabriel was knocked sideways by the blow, and the two of them fell through the gateway headfirst.

They fell into darkness, spinning out of control, the thin stream of white lights left far behind. Gabriel flapped frantically, feathers falling out left and right.

"Oh boy, oh boy! Which way is up?" Gabriel huffed, flapping his free arm and kicking his legs, too. "Pull out! Pull out! Mayday! Mayday!" he screamed. Gabriel's grip on Jamie's hand broke free, and she plunged into darkness all alone.

"If I guess what you are carrying, will you take me with you?"

CHAPTER 4

THE MAGUS*

Jamie landed on something soft with a big bump. She sat up, shook her head, and spat. She had sand in her mouth and in her ears, too. In fact, she had sand all over her. She looked around and gasped. As far as she could see there was nothing but sand in huge, rolling dunes, except for a large white star with a shimmering tail which moved slowly off in the distance like a kite.

"Gabriel! Gabriel!" Jamie shouted in every direction. There was no answer but the empty sound of the bitter winter wind. She was beginning to get scared. Her pale glow was starting to dim, and she

---

* Magician, or wise-man. The plural of magus is "magi"

was already feeling the cold. Thank goodness she'd worn her socks to bed, and that she'd hung onto her cuddly. She wrapped it around herself. She would have felt much better then, except that she had no idea where she was. She appeared to be all alone in the middle of a desert.

"Gabriel!" she hollered one more time. Just as she was about to call out again, she noticed a turbaned head appearing and disappearing over the top of one of the dunes. There it was again. And there it went again. Each time it bobbed up, she could see a bit more.

It was a man dressed in fine silken robes. By the time his waist appeared, another head appeared as well, the head of a camel.

The man rode his camel over the top of the dune and headed slowly down to a spot right in front of Jamie. He directed his camel to stop by touching the camel's head with a stick. "Hello there, little one," the man said. "I thought I heard a voice crying out in the darkness, so I came over to see. And here you are. What is your name?"

"I'm Jamie," she said. "Who are you?"

"Oh, just a wandering magus adrift in a sea of sand." The man's camel bellowed, and a most foul smell flecked with droplets of camel spittle hit Jamie's face.

"*Eww*," she said, wiping her face with her cuddly.

"Are you lost, girl? Where is your camel?"

"I didn't come by camel," Jamie said.

"Then how did you come to be here in the middle of this desert?"

"Gabriel brought me," Jamie said. "He's an angel. Only Michael bumped him, and then Gabriel dropped me. And here I am." She shrugged, and her cuddly slipped down off of one shoulder.

The magus stroked his grey but finely trimmed beard. "I have read these names in the scriptures. Indeed, even as the names of angels. But you don't look much like an angel to me, little one."

"Well, I'm not a real *real* angel," Jamie answered. "I'm only a little girl. But Gabriel is a real angel, and he was taking me to see the Christ child."

"I myself am on such a journey!" the magus exclaimed.

"Are you following the Christmas star?" Jamie asked.

"I am following a star which moves, although I do not know this name you call it by. I have read in the holy scriptures of a Messiah that is to be born under such a sign." The magus reached into his broad waistband and brought forth a scroll, which he unrolled and examined for a moment. "But I do not know *where*," he added quietly, as though talking to himself.

"In Bethlehem," Jamie said.

"Excuse me? What did you say?"

"The baby you're looking for is born in Bethlehem," Jamie said.

The magus regarded Jamie from atop his high perch. His camel was breathing down on Jamie and chewing on something gooey and foul. "I have been following this star for nearly a month, and every night I re-work the calculations. The star moves steadily toward Jerusalem."

"Bethlehem," Jamie repeated. "Trust me on this one."

"I have heard of this name, too," the magus said. "But it is not on my map. Perhaps this place is near Jerusalem. I shall go there and ask their wise men of it." He rolled up his scroll and tucked it into his belt.

Jamie remembered her father reading to her. She remembered a name. Herod. Didn't the awful King Herod live in Jerusalem? "Don't go to Jerusalem," Jamie said. "Go straight to Bethlehem."

"And which way is Bethlehem?" the magus asked. The camel made a noise that sounded like a question, too.

Jamie shrugged again, and her cuddly slipped from her other shoulder as well. She shivered and wrapped it around herself once more.

The magus sighed. "So you see my problem. I am sitting on my camel in the middle of the desert, conversing with a young slip of a girl who claims to have come down from the angels, and who directs me to travel to a place she herself cannot find." The magus shook his head as if to shoo away an insect. "I think I have been without food too long. But Jerusalem I can find." He spoke to his camel and made clicking sounds with his tongue. He tapped the camel with his stick and said, "Come, Geeza!" The camel began to turn away.

Jamie suddenly realized that in a few moments, she would be all alone again. And wherever she was, it was certainly a long way from her bedroom. And where was Gabriel? No telling when the old angel would be back. *Or if.* Jamie shivered, and not only because of the cold. "Wait!" she called out.

"What is it, my little illusion?" the magus said over his shoulder.

"Are you carrying a gift for the baby?" Jamie asked.

"Is it your business to know these things?" the magus said with uplifted eyebrows. The smell from the back end of the camel was even worse than the front, but Jamie ignored it.

She took a chance that his answer meant that the magus did indeed carry a gift. An idea lit up her face. "If I guess what you're carrying, will you take me with you?"

The magus smiled a wry smile. "You'll never guess it," he said.

"But if I do, will you?"

"Very well. Yes."

"Is it gold?" Jamie asked.

The magus laughed. "An obvious guess! But the answer will have to be, would I tell anyone if I did carry gold? No. The answer is no. I have no gold." He laughed again.

"Is it frankincense?" Jamie asked.

"An interesting guess, little one." The magus stroked his beard. "A thoughtful guess. But no, I do not carry frankincense, and time is too valuable for this game. Farewell."

"Wait!" Jamie cried out. "I know who you are! You're Gaspar, and you bring the gift of myrrh!"

The magus stared at her, and his mouth dropped open. "Dear God! How did you know this? I have told no one!"

"Let's just say I have friends in high places," Jamie grinned. "Now, will you take me with you to Bethlehem?"

"Jerusalem," the magus said. "And there we will ask the way." Gaspar turned and searched for the star. He gazed at it for a moment as it twinkled in the distance, its tail stretching down toward the distant hills as if reaching for something. Then he slowly shook his head. "I fear we'll be too late," he said.

"You won't be too late," Jamie said.

"How do you know this?"

"Because the Bible says that one of the wise-men brought myrrh to the baby Jesus." Jamie sighed, and wrinkled up her nose. "How come none of you brought toys? Don't you think he'd like a teddy-bear more? What is myrrh, anyway?" Jamie shook more sand out of her nightgown.

The old magus chuckled, but seemed to remain sad in spite of it. "This baby is very special, little one. He will be a king. But kings always manage to anger other kings, and many die young. It is the way of this world. But *this* one, he will be a king even among kings. He will be lucky to even grow up at all. I bring myrrh for his mother to place on his body, that she may mourn longer before her final kiss goodbye." Gaspar's eyes seemed to cloud for a moment, and hunched over on his camel, he seemed extremely old.

"Have you lost someone?" Jamie said in her quietest voice.

"Yes," the magus answered.

"You'll see them again," Jamie said. "I know."

The magus straightened and regarded her with widened eyes. "Can this be true?" he said.

"Sure," Jamie said, and smiled. "You get to see everybody. I just came from there."

The magus slowly smiled too. "You mend my heart, little one. Perhaps you are an angel after all. Come. Let us be on our way. We've a baby to see!" Gaspar held out his hand.

Before Jamie could take Gaspar's hand, a bright but very brief glow appeared on the other side of the camel. Jamie could see that it was Gabriel, appearing out of nowhere, his wings askew and feathers spinning. Gabriel quickly tucked in his wings and stopped glowing before Gaspar could turn around.

"Greetings and salutations, O great one," Gabriel said, bowing, but not so low as to reveal his wings. "I see you have found my, ah, grand-daughter. A thousand thanks to you. May you have as many feathers in your—*ahem*, may God favor you with ample shade and water," Gabriel corrected himself.

"And you are…?" Gaspar coaxed for an answer.

"A pardon, please. My name is Gabriel. And this is my grand-daughter, Jamie. She is a strange child." Gabriel pointed a finger at his ear and twirled it in little circles. He smiled broadly, missing teeth and all.

"She is gifted," the magus said. "Take good care of her."

"Yes, O great one," Gabriel said, bowing a little deeper this time. Jamie could see a bit of wing sticking out, but doubted that Gaspar could.

Gaspar regarded Gabriel a moment longer, then pursed his lips and put a finger to them. "Your grand-daughter wants me to take her to Jerusalem."

"Bethlehem!" Jamie corrected.

"Jamie, *shh!* She's just a child." Gabriel smiled again and shrugged apologetically. A wing almost popped out as he did so, but he held it in with one hand. "You must travel where you must go alone. I will take care of her. Come, child," Gabriel said to Jamie.

"Farewell, old man," Gaspar said. "If you are a man. This night is full of strangeness! Come, Geeza. We have many hills to climb before we dine in Jerusalem!" Gaspar clicked his tongue several times and struck his camel lightly with his stick. The camel began moving, and the magus swayed up and down until they both disappeared over the top of a nearby dune.

"Thank God, no harm was done," Gabriel exhaled loudly and began to glow again. He closed his eyes and grunted, and his wings popped out one at a time. Most of his feathers were bent in the middle. "Help me unfold these, will you?" Gabriel said.

"You told him I was your *grand-daughter*?" Jamie said.

"Well, it was either that or tell him I'm a retired archangel who borrowed you from two thousand years in the future. I thought he'd handle the grand-daughter story a bit better. Easy on the tips, Kiddo. I'm a bit more brittle than I used to be."

"It seems like you have more feathers than when I saw you last," Jamie said, unbending the biggest ones by placing a foot on Gabriel's back for leverage.

"Probably do. I've covered a lot of ground tonight. But now look, they're all bent! Merciful heavens, how I dislike tucking them in a hurry!"

"But didn't you lie to Gaspar? Jamie asked. "Can angels lie?"

"Ah, *hmm*. Well, it's not a real *real* lie," Gabriel chuckled, preening what feathers he could reach. "We are sort of related."

"We are?"

"Sure," Gabriel said, flapping his wings to test them. "If you take the word 'great', put it before grandfather, and repeat it two-to-the-thirteenth power, and then add three more for good luck, I'm related to everybody. In fact, everybody's related to everybody, if you go back that far. And in heaven, that's not so very far at all. So, grandfather, or great-grandfather-to-the-thirteenth-plus-three—what's the difference? It's how you feel in your heart that really matters." Gabriel gave Jamie a gentle hug. "And I like you every bit as much as I liked your father."

Jamie gasped. "You know my dad? Did you take him with you on Christmas Eve, too?"

"Indeed I did, and his father before him, don't you know."

"What did they get to see? Can you tell me?" Jamie asked.

"No, child. It's up to your father to tell you about his journey if he wants to. Different people see different things. Everybody sees what they need to see to illuminate their own path. I can tell you it was a good trip, though. We had fun. Tell him Old Gabe says hello when you get back home."

"I promise," Jamie said. "If you promise not to drop me on my head anymore."

"Deal," Gabriel said. "Now, let's get going. It won't do at all to be late. Hop on!" Gabriel helped Jamie to climb up in between his now mostly straightened wings. She held on to the place where they attached to his shoulders. "Next stop, Bethlehem!" Gabriel shouted, but it took him fifteen running steps to get airborne. Even so, Jamie's feet hit the top of the first dune they flew over.

"Gabriel, I have some questions," Jamie said.

"Okay shoot, Kiddo, but make it quick," Gabriel huffed.

"How come I could understand Gaspar? How did he know English?"

Gabriel chuckled. "He didn't. It's just part of the blessing of being an angel. Angels understand everybody, and everybody understands angels. Ever hear of an angel that didn't speak the right language?"

"No," Jamie said.

"Well, there you have it," Gabriel said.

"Gabriel, I have another question," Jamie said. "How come Gaspar's going to Jerusalem when Jesus was born in Bethlehem?"

"*Is going* to be," Gabriel said. "Not *was*. We're a couple of days early yet." Gabriel huffed and wheezed as he flew. "And Gaspar is destined to speak to King Herod. You mustn't go trying to change things around. Things have to turn out just so, and angels are strictly forbidden to interfere in the ways of man."

"But *you're* interfering with *me!*" Jamie said.

"Well, I'm an archangel, Kiddo. Archangels can interfere," Gabriel held out his hand with a thumb and a finger close together. "Maybe just a little. But there's tons of paperwork involved. Who would have thought so many lawyers would actually go to heaven?" Gabriel shook his head. "It's why I retired."

"But you're not a real *real* archangel anymore, are you?" Jamie said.

"Well, no, but I still have my union card. Wanna see?" Gabriel reached into his robe and started searching around, but his uneven motions made the ride extremely bumpy for Jamie, who screamed.

"That's okay! I believe you!" Jamie said in a louder and higher than normal voice.

"Sorry," Gabriel said. "Anyway, thank God I found you before the angel glow wore off."

"What if it had?" Jamie held on as tight as she could with one hand, her cuddly streaming behind in the other.

"Well, for one thing, you'd have been a lot harder to find. You gave me quite a scare!"

"*You* were scared, hah! I was *lost!*" Jamie said.

"You were *misplaced*, Kiddo. We don't use the L-word in heaven. Anyway, from now on, follow my advice: Hold onto me all the time, don't go talking with strangers, and don't go messing with anything."

Jamie sighed. "That's what my mom says to me when we go shopping at Macy's," she said.

"Well, no harm done this time," Gabriel said. "Actually, I think you cheered him up a bit, although sadness still follows him like a shadow. You did good, Jamie."

"Do I get a feather then?" Jamie asked.

"I don't think so. You aren't a real *real* angel yet. But you'll get your feathers one day, I have no doubt. Now fasten your seatbelt, Kiddo!"

Just as Jamie said, "What seatbelt?" Gabriel's wings took one mighty (although not completely even) flap, and suddenly they were no longer over a desert. Jamie saw low, rolling hills spotted with dark green dots. In the dim light, the thin, scraggly bushes looked like stubble on an old man's face.

Up ahead, the Christmas star shimmered brightly, its sinuous tail almost touching a nearby hilltop but passing over it instead. Gabriel crested the same hilltop a moment after and glided down the star-brightened slope toward a thin grove of trees in the gully below. Jamie could see the star's tail plainly now, a crowded swarm of circles filled with wings.

"Ahh, all caught up, and almost time. *Whew!*" Gabriel huffed. Suddenly, a double trumpet note filled the night from above. "Hah! Now it *is* time!" Gabriel said. But under his breath, Jamie could just barely hear him also say, *"I need to see if you're ready yet!"*

"What? Are you talking to me?" Jamie asked as they passed over the grove of trees. She could see a tiny pond beyond the trees.

Gabriel shook his head, but before he could say anything more, the star's tail passed directly over the top of them, and Jamie could hear hundreds of voices singing and pointing.

"It's time! It's time!" Many of the angels shouted all at once. In the blink of an eye, the tail of the star seemed to lash out across the sky like a whip.

"Hang on!" Gabriel shouted, but he was spun upside-down by the force of it. His wings beat frantically, and Jamie lost her grip on them. In the wing-wash from a thousand angels, Jamie was suddenly falling, and Gabriel was gone.

She landed in a field of grass stubble and rolled to a stop beneath a thin, scraggly tree. The Christmas star had finally touched down on the far side of the small pond, on the slope of the next hill, perhaps half a mile away.

"Harumph," John said. "You don't look much like an angel."

CHAPTER 5

TWO BOYS AND A DOG

Jamie sat up and looked around her. She was sitting among thin clumps of brown grass. Short stalks of it were poking her through her nightgown, and she had grass in her hair. In the pale light of her already fading angel glow, she could see that the edges of the field were not very far away. *Some of the rich kids at school had lawns bigger than this*, she thought. Here and there, she could see scruffy little trees with hard grey bark and tiny leaves. And on the ground beneath the trees, little black dots. Jamie picked one up; it was an olive.

Jamie loved olives. She bit off one end of the olive, pried out the pit, and stuck a finger inside.

She repeated this until all of her fingers and thumb on her right hand were wearing little olive caps. As she reached for another from a big pile of olives, she noticed that these were covered with flies—and smelled awful. It was then that she heard the bleating of sheep, and a dog barking off in the darkness.

"*Eww*," she said. She decided *not* to gather any more olives. But before she could take the others off her fingers, she saw a face peering out at her from behind a nearby tree. It was a boy not very much older than she. The boy revealed a disheveled mass of black hair, and the top of a heavy woolen shirt. "Who are you?" she asked.

"I was here first," the boy said, his voice quivering with uncertainty. "Who are *you?*"

"I'm Jamie," Jamie said, but then she remembered what Gabriel had told her. "I'm not supposed to talk to strangers," she added.

"Me neither," the boy said. "But then, what are you doing in the middle of my field?"

"I fell off an angel," Jamie said.

"You *what?*" The boy inserted a finger into his ear and turned it back and forth.

"I just dropped in to say hello," Jamie said, trying to be friendly and not at all scared. "What's your name?"

"I'm John, son of Zacharius," the boy said. "And you are scaring my sheep. Some of them have gone into the water."

"I'm very sorry," Jamie said. "I didn't mean to scare your sheep."

"What makes you shine so?" John asked.

"I'm an angel, kind of *sort* of," Jamie said.

"You don't look much like an angel," John said.

"That's what people keep telling me," Jamie sighed.

"My father says *real* angels are bigger, and have wings," John said. He came out from behind the tree a little bit, but not all the way. Jamie could see that he had no pants on—only leggings wrapped in leather thongs from his sandals. Fortunately, John's shirt extended all the way down to his knees.

"Has your father seen lots of angels?" Jamie asked.

John shrugged. "My father's kind of strange sometimes. You never know with him."

"Well then, there you have it!" Jamie said.

"There I have what?" John said.

"I *could* be an angel then," Jamie said. She noticed, though, that her angel glow was fading fast.

"I don't think so," John said.

"Could *too*," Jamie said.

"Not," John answered.

"Too!"

"Not!"

"*Hmph!*" Jamie snorted. This wasn't at all how the story went when her dad read it. "Look, John, I'm not a real *real* angel, but a real angel brought me here. Actually, we weren't coming *here* here, we were going over *there*." Jamie pointed to where the Christmas star had touched down, but she noticed that John didn't even glance in that direction. He was staring at her with widened eyes. "Can't you come out and talk with me? I can explain everything," she added.

"I don't think so," John said. "You're starting to remind me of my father after he's been to the temple—all this talk about angels!"

"You don't need to be afraid," Jamie said. "I have wonderful news!"

"I can go home now and crawl into bed by the hearth-fire?" John asked, sounding very much like that would be the best news he could possibly hear.

"Even better than that, John," Jamie smiled. "Tonight, in Bethlehem, a special baby is being born right now! His name is Jesus, and he's going to be the mess… the messy…" Jamie was drawing a blank. "What is that M-word, anyway?"

"My father talks about a Messiah," John said. "Is that the word?"

"Yes! That's it!" Jamie said.

"So, let me get this straight," John said. "You're saying that the Messiah is being born right here in this little inky-dinky no-where town, right here, right tonight?" John's eyebrows went up for just a moment, but then he frowned and shook his head. "I don't think so," he said. "I may be a country boy, but I wasn't born yesterday!"

"Please believe me, John!" Jamie held out her hand toward him, but was embarrassed to see that her fingers were still wearing their little olive hats. She quickly drew it back.

"Are you selling something?" John said. We don't have any money, you know. I don't think either of us would be shepherds if we—"

"*We?*" Jamie looked around, but it was too dark to see anyone.

John hollered over his shoulder. "Jacob!"

An older boy approached out of the darkness. He looked a lot like John, except his face was leaner and more muscular, his tousled hair a bit longer, and his leggings were dripping wet. "What is it?" the older boy said. "Can't you see I'm busy? The sheep are mired in the mud by the spring. Little Three-Legs almost drowned!"

"This is my cousin, Jacob," John said.

"Who is this girl?" Jacob said, pointing at Jamie. Jamie's angel glow was almost gone. "Are you the one that scared my sheep?" Jacob looked very angry.

"This is Jamie," John said. "She says she's an angel. She says that the Messiah is being born in Bethlehem tonight."

"Uh-huh," Jacob said, thin lipped. "*Right.* And I'm Herod's nephew, and Dog is an angel, too." Jacob turned and walked into the darkness. Jamie heard Jacob's voice calling, "Dog! Hey, Dog!" She heard him whistle, and then he reappeared again. "I think you'd better go now, girl," he said. "You've scared my sheep, and I don't think Dog will like you very much."

"Wait, you've got to believe me!" Jamie said, trying to remember the Christmas story that she hadn't listened to very closely. She was a bit sorry now. *What was it that she was supposed to say? Lindsey had known it. Oh yes!* "Go see for yourself! You'll find the baby wrapped in swaddling clothes, and lying in a manger. Trust me on this," Jamie said.

"That doesn't sound very Messiah-like," Jacob said. "And you don't look very angel-like either." Jacob turned away, and then turned back to Jamie, his frown changing into a distinctly unfriendly grin. "Let's see what Dog thinks," he added. Jamie heard a low growl and suddenly saw two slits of eyes. They belonged to a very large, very mean looking black dog.

"The fact is," Jacob smiled a very cat-playing-with-a-mouse-like smile, "…to Dog, you're a sheep-scarer. That means you look a lot more like a wolf to him than an angel. And Dog doesn't much like wolves, do you, Dog?" The growling grew louder and the big dog lunged forward, but Jacob caught him by the scruff of his neck. "Now, if I were to just say the word 'wolf' and then let go…"

Jamie pulled her legs in and started scooting backwards like a crab. "Nice doggy! Gooood doggy!" she said quietly, followed immediately by, "*Gabriel!*"

Jacob was not through with her, it seemed. He untied a leather strap from around his waist and looped it over Dog's head. "*Wolf,*" he said into Dog's ear, and let some of the strap slide through his hand at the same time. Dog surged forward with fangs bared, making a growl that was more like a roar than any dog-sound Jamie had ever heard. "Get out of my field," Jacob said.

"Please, you've got to believe me!" Jamie said, her voice quivering with fright.

"*Wolf,*" Jacob said, and Dog surged forward again.

"I didn't do anything bad!" Jamie whimpered.

"Wolf, wolf, *wolf*!" Jacob taunted, and each time, Dog lunged at Jamie. Jamie scooted backwards as fast as she could push with her feet, but Dog's teeth snapped onto the corner of her cuddly. Jamie screamed and pulled as hard as she could, but Dog held on tight until a piece of the corner ripped away.

"Go away, you mean old dog!" Jamie cried, but Dog did not go away. His head lowered and his fangs bared, he began to pull Jacob forward by his leash.

"Some angel *you* are," Jacob said, laughing. "*Wolf*, Dog! Get the *wolf*!"

Just as Dog lunged forward, Gabriel appeared in a flash of light, his wings almost fully feathered, directly between Jamie and Dog. He bent down into the startled dog's face, his wings fully extended, and said, "Not wolf. More like an eagle. Only with *fangs*!" Gabriel smiled, a glint of light revealing a few more teeth than he normally had. Dog's eyes went very wide; his lips formed a little "O" just under his nose, and a tiny little whine came out. Then Dog ran between Jacob's legs, pulling the strap from his master's hands, and disappeared into the darkness. Jacob dropped to his knees and then bent his face straight down into the ground. John hid behind his tree again.

"Gabriel! Am I glad to see *you*!" Jamie said, drying her eyes with the clean end of her cuddly. She examined the other end; at least the piece that was torn away was smaller than her hand. "Where have you *been?*" she said.

"There are many fields, and many shepherds," Gabriel replied.

"Your wings—they're beautiful!" Jamie said.

"I've been pulling sheep out of the water from here to Jerusalem," Gabriel said. "It's funny how time stands still when you're having a good time. But I truly believe this is the last field." Gabriel cleared his throat, a process that took longer than Jamie would have thought polite. "*Ahemmm*," he began. "Fear not, for behold, I bring you tidings of great joy, which shall be to all people…"

"I already told them that," Jamie said.

"You did?" Gabriel frowned. "That was supposed to be my job." He shrugged, moving up and down in the air as his wings moved. "Oh well. Did you tell them about the manger and the swaddling cloth?"

"Swaddling clothes," Jamie corrected.

"Cloth," Gabriel said.

"The Bible says *clothes*," Jamie said.

"Look, Kiddo, it's swaddling cloth. They're just rags, not clothes. They didn't have—well, you'll see. 'Clothes' is a misprint," Gabriel said.

"A *misprint*? In the *Bible*?"

"Well, I know Luke, and he said *cloth*!" Gabriel was frowning and trying to re-light his cigar from his own halo without using either hand. "It got changed when it was written down so many years later," he added.

Jacob was looking up at him with a puzzled look, pieces of grass stubble stuck to his face. "Are you God?" he asked timidly.

Gabriel snorted, a new puff of smoke coming from his mouth. The smoke curled into a perfect "O" above his head, like a second halo. "No, I'm not God, boy. I'm not anything like God. Actually, the closest you'll ever get to understanding what God looks like is to go see a certain baby over there in

Bethlehem. He's about, let's see…" Gabriel looked at his duct-taped hourglass. "He's about twelve minutes old right now." Gabriel motioned with a hand toward the star. "Follow the crowds. Angels everywhere. Can't miss it."

"But the sheep—"Jacob said.

"They'll be alright. I'll see to it." Gabriel unhooked his peculiar trumpet and blew a riff of trumpet notes. Suddenly, angels swooped down from every direction. "Over here!" One yelled, and others motioned. More came until the sky was filled with them. Many were singing, *"Ju – bil – la – te, dey – o, Ha – le – lu – jah!"* Gabriel gestured upwards and then sideways, and two of the angels streaked down toward the spring. One of the last blank places in Gabriel's left wing filled in with a beautiful feather. "Believe it with all your heart, for all you have heard is true. Go and see," Gabriel said to Jacob.

"Can I go too?" John's voice quivered from behind his tree.

"This matter is up to your cousin, John," Gabriel smiled. "But it would be a great blessing for you both if he were to take you along."

John came out from behind his tree, but not all the way. "How did you know my name?"

Gabriel mimicked John's voice. *"I may be a country angel, but I wasn't born yesterday!"* Then his own voice returned. "Angels know a lot of things. Now, go on, both of you!"

Gabriel reached out to Jamie. "Your glow is almost gone, Kiddo. You need a recharge. Here, take my hand."

Jamie took Gabriel's hand in hers, and she began to glow anew, as bright as the other angels. A feeling of peace and safety flooded over her like warmth from a hot water bottle. She smiled and said, *"Ahhh."*

"See, I told you, Kiddo. Angels never use the L-word." Gabriel started to rise off the ground, pulling Jamie gently along with him. "Just a minute," he said, looking over his shoulder at Jacob, who was still kneeling in the grass. "I have one more thing to say. I want you boys to remember it and to tell your grandchildren about it one day." Gabriel took a big breath, and then his voice came out loud and deep, resonating from everywhere at once. **"Glory** *to God in the Highest, and on earth, peace, goodwill toward men.*"

Gabriel made a gesture like sweeping, and drew his hand from the boys toward the town, his hand coming to rest on his stomach. His cheeks filled up, but no sound came out. He exhaled quickly, and whispered to Jamie, "Excuse me. It upsets my tummy to talk like that anymore. Michael is so much better at it. Say, you didn't say the glory to God part yet, did you?"

"No," Jamie said. "I forgot."

"Good. It's my best line. Took a lot of re-writing to get it just so. It's kind of my personal gift to Christmas, don't you know." Gabriel started to rise again, pulling Jamie after him. "Get going, boys! What d'ya want, *tickets*?"

"I'm sorry I scared your sheep," Jamie called down over her shoulder. She could see both boys still staring at them, their mouths agape, grass stubble stuck to their cheeks.

"Don't worry about it," Gabriel whispered to her. "Everything turns out just fine."

"I did okay then?" Jamie asked.

"You did good, Kiddo," Gabriel said. "But in this business, everything works together for good in the long run. Of course, *long*, to someone like me, might be a millennium or two." Gabriel chuckled. "But I think *long*, to Dog, is going to be the rest of the night!"

"I didn't mean to cause any trouble," Jamie said.

"You didn't. Minor paperwork. No problem," Gabriel said.

Somehow, Jamie didn't feel much better. Scaring the wits out of people was not considered very good manners at her house. She had been pretty embarrassed by the whole thing. In fact, now that she thought about it, she was rather tired and miserable. Her arms hurt from being pulled along at only God knew what speed, her backside ached from falling on it from only God knew how high, and she had sand in her socks. Not to mention nearly being a midnight snack for a huge snarling dog! All in all, traveling by angel was not nearly as preferable as traveling by school bus. Jamie missed her home, her mom and dad, and her own warm bed. She even missed her sister— only a little, though. Suddenly, she felt a very long ways away from all of that, and a tear stung her eyes. She snuffled the next few back, and said, "Gabriel, I want to go *home!*"

Gabriel pulled her close and gave her a gentle hug. "There, there," he said softly. "I can run you home any time you want to go, Kiddo. But I'd like you to meet a friend of mine first."

"I'm *so* tired," Jamie said. She held her cuddly close to her face, snuggled into it, and wiped her tears away with a good corner. "I'm not sure I want to meet any more of your friends."

"But she's a very special person, Jamie."

"She who?"

"Her name is Mary," Gabriel said.

"Mary?" Jamie gasped. *The* Mary?"

"Yes, Mary, brand new mother of a very special child." Gabriel smiled. "Be brave for just a little while longer, Kiddo, and I'll show you something you'll not soon forget. But you must truly want to see it with all your heart, or else we'll be homeward bound."

Jamie sighed. She had come so far already, and she was so close. She would be brave a little longer.

Jamie grinned, her tiredness gone. "I do," she said firmly.

"That's the spirit! Okay, then. Better climb up on top and hang on." Gabriel swung her up onto his back between his wings, and Jamie put her arms around his neck and held on tight this time. No more falling for *her*!

They started to move upward and slightly toward the star. Gabriel began to hum the same music as Jamie could hear the angels singing off in the distance. Then Gabriel patted Jamie's arm around his neck. "*Ahem*—ease up a little, Kiddo. You're making me into a soprano."

"Sorry, Gabe." Jamie loosened her grip a tiny bit, but not too much.

Gabriel glanced at his hourglass. "We're a tad bit late. Not real *real* late, but see, I like to be at the head of the line."

Jamie pictured the lunch line at school. "Me too," she said. "What line?"

"The line to see the new baby, of course!" Gabriel said. "I need to be in the front so I can see if Mary is ready for visitors yet. It wouldn't do to have everybody popping in too early. I promised her that if angels came, they wouldn't come until she said she was ready. And it's my job to look out for her."

"Like a guardian angel, kind of sort of?" Jamie said.

"Exactly. And of *course* I said 'yes.'"

"You were Mary's guardian angel?" Jamie asked.

"Still am. Present tense, remember?" Gabriel's voice became deeply resonant, but different than his everywhere-at-once kind of voice. "*'Go down and tell her she's going to have a baby,'* God said. And of course I do it." Gabriel's voice then raised an octave. "*But I'm a virgin!*' Mary says. So I say, 'Listen. In this business, anything can happen; I'm just delivering a message.' That was the hardest part. She was really scared at first…"

"Did you take Mary on any trips with you?" Jamie asked.

"That's how I cheered her up," Gabriel said.

"Where did you take her?"

"That's kind of a secret," Gabriel cautioned. "It's not quite polite to talk about what happens with other people. Everybody needs to find their own way, like I told you. But I can say this much. I didn't take Mary back to see the first Christmas night!" Gabriel chuckled at his own joke.

"Where would Mary go then?" Jamie said quietly, mostly to herself. "Can't be anything from the New Testament... I know where I'd go if I were her. Next to the Christmas story, my favorite part is the 23rd Psalm. I'd go meet the guy that wrote it. That's where *I'd* go."

Gabriel laughed so hard that Jamie had to hold on tight not to fall off his back. "Jamie, you bring tears to my eyes, girl. You're just like Mary in your heart! You'd be good friends, if we stayed long. But we can't. She and Joseph are having a really hard day. Don't be too quick to judge them by it."

"I won't."

"And stay close. Sometimes it's a bit crowded in the front."

"I will."

"If there's any pushing or shoving, just back away," Gabriel said. "No fighting. That's strictly forbidden among angels."

"I won't."

"And don't take any souvenirs, either. God knows these people don't have very much as it is, and everything that's there is supposed to be there. Leave everything alone. And don't talk to any more people." Gabriel turned so that Jamie could see his face, and made a zipping-of-the-lip movement across his closed lips with his finger and thumb.

"I will. I mean, I won't…" Jamie sighed. "Now I'm confused!"

"Never mind. Just hang onto me and you'll be fine," Gabriel said.

"You won't let go of me, will you? You won't leave me alone again?"

"I won't. I promise," Gabriel said.

"Good!" Jamie hugged him fiercely.

Gabriel made a disgusting sound, and tapped Jamie on the wrist. "Ease up a bit, Kiddo. Gotta have wind for my horn."

"Sorry."

Gabriel glanced at his hourglass and then motioned quickly to the other angels with him. "We're a tad bit late so we mustn't dawdle now. Hang on, Kiddo!"

"I will," Jamie said, followed by "*Whoa!*" as Gabriel flapped his powerful new wings, and she almost lost her grip.

Suddenly there was a town below them—short square buildings with flat roofs, all the same color as the earth between them. But Gabriel and the others did not fly down among the buildings. Instead, they flew straight over, toward the stony bluff of a hill just beyond the last house. At the base of the bluff, Jamie could see the mouth of a grotto with a rough wooden canopy built in front of it. And high above, from as far as Jamie could see, an endless stream of angels spiraling down from the Christmas star, singing and pointing at the dark opening below the canopy.

"Oh, look at that! There's already crowding up front!"

CHAPTER 6

PRESIDENTS AND KINGS

By the time Gabriel touched down in front of the entrance to the grotto, hundreds of angels had already landed. More were landing every second. Several angels had reached the edge of the canopy and were trying to peer into the dark entrance. Jamie noticed that most of the angels up in front were wingless, and she also thought she saw some pushing and shoving among them.

Gabriel helped Jamie down off his back. He put his hands on his waist, and Jamie held onto his arm. "Oh, look at that," Gabriel muttered, shaking his head. "The heads of state are at it again. They always have to be in the front of everything. 'Let's do this,' they say, and 'We'll need that.' But it's always just about themselves. *Humph*! Almost everything they do needs fixing!" he said. "Well, let's get on up there. It may be a bit early for visitors yet. I promised Mary not to allow anyone in until she says it's okay, and I *always* keep my promises." Gabriel started moving toward the grotto, stepping around angels when he could, and moving others gently aside.

"Excuse me, pardon me," Gabriel repeated several times. But as the crowd grew thicker, he started saying, "Make way, coming through!" He was less gentle then, and he pulled Jamie after him in rough jerks.

Jamie looked about her, wide-eyed among so many angels. Some of them even looked familiar. She saw a dark-haired angel with long sideburns. He was wearing a sequined shirt with a high collar and had a towel wrapped around his neck. Jamie gasped. "Gabriel," she whispered, pointing. "Is that —"

"Yes, yes. Hello, Big Guy. Still taking care of business?" Gabriel asked.

"I came to sing for the little momma," the man said.

"Fine. Join the singers over there above the canopy. Tell George Frederick that Gabriel says to put you in the front line."

"Ah well, I only do solos."

"Yes, but a *spiritual* path is one of harmony. It's best you learn to join in here. After all, this isn't *your* gig. Well, gotta go now. One side up there! Make way!" Gabriel said, pulling Jamie along after him.

They moved along, dodging around and darting in, until Gabriel almost tripped over a short, thin little man with a bald head and thick glasses.

"Mahatma!" Gabriel bowed, holding his palms together in front of his chest. "I thought you were Hindu."

"I am," Gandhi said and then continued to speak, his accent confusing whether or not this was the same sentence. "Not so very different. It seems that all paths that seek God, if sincere, have much in common."

"Well, of course they do," Gabriel said. "They all lead to the same place."

"*Ahh*, I thought so," Gandhi said. "But then why do they have so many different names?"

"They're like the facets of a jewel, Mahatma," Gabriel said. "But God will meet you halfway down *any* path as long as you seek Him." He glanced at his hourglass. "Can't chat any longer. Gotta go." Gabriel started moving forward again. Make way, coming through! Hey, down in front! No flapping!"

Jamie heard loud voices, and one very stately voice above all the others which kept saying, "Stand back! Stand back, I say!" But she couldn't see the front of the line through all the tall angels and waving wings.

Gabriel pushed his way through the crowd of angels, moving so fast that Jamie was jerked off her feet several times. But toward the front of the line, the angels were pressed together so tightly that the two of them had a difficult time moving through them at all. Jamie was jostled against a young angel with a box tied in front of him.

"Coffee, hot dogs, angel-food cake!" the young angel called out several times.

Finally, Gabriel had to slow down. "Make way!" he said loudly. He tried to push between two angels who were in the very front, just at the edge of the canopy. But the two young-looking, handsome angels moved closer together, blocking his way. Gabriel tried to go around them, but they took hold of his arms and stopped him. "Excuse me, boys. I really need to get by here," Gabriel said.

"Can't let anyone through. Official embargo," the elder of the two angels said with a distinctly Bostonian accent.

"Just following orders of the Commander-in-Chief there," the younger angel said, motioning behind himself with his head. Jamie couldn't help but notice a resemblance between the two.

"Now look, John, Bobby," Gabriel said, sweeping their arms away. "I'm on official celestial business, and I don't have time for politics."

Gabriel stepped free of the two men, but was stopped short by a third. When Gabriel tried to excuse himself and step around, the heavily bearded, cigar smoking man grabbed him by the front of his robe and lifted him up off of the ground.

"Crowding, ay?" the angry bearded man said. His breath was foul. Even Jamie could tell this angel had been drinking. "Who in the H-word do you think you are?" The angry man gestured sideways with his chin, and began talking out of the side of his mouth. "Must be a Johnny Reb! Boys, rally 'round yer General!"

In a moment, Gabriel had big burly angels holding him fast—one by each wing, one by each arm, and the angry bearded man was holding Gabriel so high that Jamie had trouble hanging onto his arm.

The two of them regarded one another face to face, each with tight lips and jaws clenched around the stubs of their cigars. Smoke rings rose in pairs. Gabriel spoke slowly around his cigar. "Well, well, Ulysses. Ever the gracious diplomat, I see."

"Let him through," a tall bearded man wearing a stovepipe hat said. "It's Gabriel."

"Thanks, Abe," Gabriel said. "Well, at least *one* of our presidents has read the Bible."

The foul-breathed man let go of Gabriel, and the others stepped back, too. A path opened through the crowd, and suddenly Jamie could see a white-haired man wearing a three-cornered hat holding up his hands in front of a muscular looking black-bearded man wearing a golden crown.

"Is that you, Gabriel?" the white-haired man said. Jamie recognized his voice as the one she had heard earlier. "Thank God, I prayed that someone would come. I've just tried to establish a little order here, a line perhaps. But King David's group won't listen."

"Is that the David that wrote the Psalms?" Jamie whispered to Gabriel.

"The same," Gabriel whispered back. "But he was much younger then, and unspoiled by being a king." The old angel sighed and shook his head.

The white-haired man turned to King David. "Let's let a higher authority decide," he said with a smile.

"I *am* a higher authority!" King David said.

Gabriel pulled Jamie along the path and stepped to the front of the crowd. Jamie could see the white-haired man closely now, and recognized him from his picture on the middle of a dollar bill.

"Thank you, George. I should have expected to see you taking command of the situation. You've done well, but I'll take it from here." Gabriel turned toward King David, who was closely followed by several younger angels. "Now, let's all calm down!" Gabriel said, holding up his free hand. "You'll all get a chance to see. I'll just take a quick peek and see if Mary's ready for visitors."

"The prophets have promised this special babe to the House of David for a thousand years. I'm eager to see my offspring," King David said.

"This baby doesn't belong to just your clan. He belongs to everybody." Gabriel spoke softly, his free hand palm outward in front of him. "Have patience, your highness."

"But I intend to see *now*!" King David said slowly and loudly.

Jamie couldn't help but notice that while his voice wasn't exactly heard everywhere at once, everyone in the crowd of angels had suddenly stopped fidgeting to listen.

"*Humph!*" Gabriel snorted. "People that think they're *special!*" he muttered to himself and shook his head again. He slicked back his hair and then held out both hands palm outward toward the king. "What is it about you front-liners that makes you think the common courtesies the rest of us live by don't apply to you? It's no wonder none of you have any wings!"

A younger man stepped up beside King David. "Let me get a word in," he said, holding up an arm in front of the king. "Listen, I have a substantial sum hidden away. You just let us go in first, and I'll make this baby the richest Messiah the world will ever know."

"This baby is already rich far beyond your understanding," Gabriel said.

King David moved the younger man's arm away. "Never mind, son. Bargaining with these holier-than-thou types is a waste of time. I mean to see my offspring right now, and that's that! Stand aside, Gabriel!" King David's voice was lower, and his brow was furled into a scowl. "God has always blessed me with His favor, and I believe He wants me to have first peek. I claim it as my right. And if you interfere, there's going to be trouble. My ancestors have wrestled with angels before, and with notable success, I might add. Time to see if my clan still has what it takes!"

King David started toward Gabriel, his teeth clenched into a tight snarl. But before he had gone two steps, a slender man with long stringy hair wearing wire-rimmed glasses gently grasped his shoulder, preventing him from taking another step.

"Give peace a chance," the man with the wire-rimmed glasses said to King David.

"Who are you, you little pip-squeak?" David said, giving the man a mighty shove.

Jamie hid behind Gabriel's wing.

"John, are you all right?" Gabriel said. "Better get over with the other singers."

Then Gabriel held up his hand toward the king. "Now see here, David! Let's not get rude. You're scaring the children!" Gabriel turned sideways and spoke over Jamie's head. "Excuse me. I knew I'd find you near the presidents. Listen, take care of the girl for just a minute, won't you dear?" Jamie felt her hand being passed to another, softer hand. She turned and stared at her temporary new guardian, a blonde-haired woman who had trouble keeping her dress down in the wind from all the angel wings.

"Are you a movie star?" Jamie asked.

"*Shh*, honey," the woman said. "I think we better step back a little. The boss looks *mad*."

"God's will be done!" King David said, starting forward again.

"*Hey* now," Gabriel held both hands up again. "Work with me here, David! You've got to get with the program! God's will isn't something you can put on like a shirt. To assume it is the height of arrogance. You'll never get a single feather that way. A spiritual path is about joining into the group, about feeling what others feel, about putting their needs before your own. Now Mary, see, she's asked that—"

"Get out of the way!" King David said, raising his arm in anger.

"You leave Gabriel alone, you big bully!" Jamie screamed in her loudest voice. "You're a big..." she closed her eyes to think of just the right awful word. "Disappointment!" she said, stamping her foot at the same time. Tears came, but she snuffled them back and decided to be more angry than afraid.

Gabriel glanced over at her. "Don't bother, child." The old angel muttered. "Special people don't listen very well, either."

King David regarded the two of them for a moment and then swept the back of his hand at them. "Bah!" he said and strode toward the canopy.

Gabriel stepped into David's path. The king reached out to push the old angel the same as he had the man with the wire-rimmed glasses, but Gabriel turned sideways and guided him into a headfirst fall. King David's crown went rolling like a runaway frisbee.

"Well, Dave," Gabriel snickered. "It looks like God wanted you to fall on your head!" He turned toward Jamie. "Got a new teacher. He calls it *Aikido*." Gabriel grinned and shrugged just as a large number of his new feathers fell out, and many of the ones remaining went askew.

King David sat up and shook his head as though trying to get water out of his ears. Then he made a gesture toward the men bunched up behind him. "Samson? Samson! Take him out!"

A huge, heavily muscled man with long, dark hair down to the middle of his back carrying a bone club stepped out of the crowd behind King David. He grinned in a most unfriendly way and began to stride confidently toward Gabriel.

"A ringer, ay?" Gabriel said. "Well, two can play that game. Can some of you help me out here?"

Two slender, wiry Asian men dressed in black leapt over Gabriel and handsprung to a spot directly in front of Samson. Samson patted his bone club against his free hand. The older of the two Asian men pulled out a pair of scissors and growled like a cat. The three men began to circle each other, crouching down into fighting stances.

Suddenly there was thunder and lightning, and a bright light began to grow in between Samson and the Asian men. The light expanded into a circle much larger than all of them, forcing them back. Then a humongous pair of wings unfolded out of the light.

"Boys, boys, here now!" Michael's voice echoed out of the light and was heard everywhere at once. **"See how fighting escalates? You know the rules!"**

"Sorry, Mike," Gabriel said. "But I didn't actually hit anybody this time."

"Now see here! You know that the message of this baby's life is going to be to help and to heal and to love one another, don't you?"

Jamie could see that Michael was pointing a gnarled finger at Gabriel, but the finger was bent with age and actually pointed at her. Gabriel and she both nodded at the same time.

"I expect you to remember in the future that fighting represents *failure*," Michael said. Then the archangel turned to the crowd, his voice echoing everywhere at once again. **"Now, pay attention! I'm putting Gabriel in charge of Christmas. Obey him. Don't make me come back!"** Michael gave a double blast on his long horn, and an open boat with a single mast and sail appeared alongside his circle of light. The archangel stepped in, with the aid of several habit-clad women to hold up his wings, and sat in the stern of the boat. "Trim the sail, sisters. I've got places to go!" Michael motioned forward with his hand, and said, "Halle- luuu, *jah!*" On the last syllable, the boat, the archangel, and the bright light all disappeared in a lightning flash and a clap of thunder.

Amid the gasps, whispering, and the flapping of wings, Jamie could barely find the king. David and all his followers had joined the others in bowing so low that she could not see their faces.

"Now look at the mess you've made of things!" Gabriel wagged a bent finger in King David's general direction, and a dozen angels cringed. "I was almost done, too. Some of this stuff gets written down, don't you know. How would it look a millennium or two from now when a father sits down to read the Christmas story to his children, and the Holy Scripture reads, 'And suddenly there appeared a multitude of heavenly hosts, praising God in the highest, bickering and fighting for vantage points...?' This is going to take some serious editing." Gabriel shook his head. "You've got to remember your basics, David. Courtesy and respect. And a pinch of patience wouldn't hurt either. Everything we do is painted like a signboard across the universe, don't you know."

King David spoke softly, with his eyes averted downward. "I've been bad, haven't I?"

Gabriel sighed. "How come no one believes the truth unless it comes with thunder and lightning?" The old angel shrugged, his tattered wings moving up and down as he did so.

"I've been a, just an, um…" The king struggled for the right word.

"Butthead," Gabriel said. Jamie giggled in spite of her tears. *"Made you smile,"* Gabriel whispered to her.

"Really!" King David's eyebrow went up on one side, but then both of them joined in a contrite double slant. "I have, haven't I? Forgive me."

"Forgive you, ah, *what?*" Gabriel coaxed.

"Please. Forgive me please." King David sighed.

"Oh, all right. I'm such a pushover," Gabriel said.

"Thank you," King David said.

"You're welcome, but don't forget that the subject may come up later, higher up. You might want to pray about it. In fact, that would be an excellent way for all of us to celebrate our togetherness." Gabriel paused and cleared his throat with a disgusting sound. **"Now that we are together,"** Gabriel spoke in a loud, clear voice which was heard everywhere at once. He placed his palms together in front of his chest and looked directly at King David.

King David sighed again and slowly bowed his head. "Why must I learn all my lessons the hard way?"

"Because you're a poet. You must take the truth deeper into your heart than others," Gabriel said softly. "**Now, *shh!***" Gabriel waited until everyone had put their hands together in front of them. "**Calm yourselves for a moment and pray, in whatever manner you choose, for the greatest good to come about.**" Gabriel paused, his cheeks fill up with air, and a little burp came out. "Excuse me," he said quietly.

Gabriel walked over to Jamie and took her hand from the blonde woman's. "Got an antacid?" Gabriel sighed. "I gotta get a desk job. Maybe I should retire again. Oh, well. Come with me, child." The old angel pulled Jamie by the hand to the base of the bluff near the canopy. "I've arranged for a little bit of music while I check on the new mother," Gabriel said, his voice loud enough to hear by all those near him, but not everywhere at once. Jamie thought his voice seemed a little hoarse now, and the old angel appeared tired, too. But Gabriel smiled, looked upward, and waved. "Ready, George Frederick? Take it away!" he shouted, grinning. Gabriel looked down at Jamie and blew a perfect smoke ring over her head.

"What were you looking at?" Jamie whispered to Gabriel. She peeked upwards around the edge of the canopy and saw thousands of angels gathering into gently arcing chorus lines. She could only see the front; rows and rows of angels extended backwards for as far as she could see, up and over the top of the bluff. She recognized several of the faces in the front from the pictures on her dad's old records. She noticed the choir director, who had his back to her, had very long white hair, and had only a single feather in each wing. She also noticed one face about three rows back which looked very familiar. *Was that her father?* No, couldn't be. Way too young.

But before she could get a better look, Gabriel pulled her underneath the canopy.

"Better duck in here, child," he said. "This could be a bit, well, *exuberant*."

Suddenly, several thousand voices rang out, clearer and louder than a thunderstorm. *"Hal - le - lu - jah! Hal - le - lu - jah! Hal - le - lu - u - u - jah!"*

The force of the music knocked the few people still standing to their knees. There were loud gasps everywhere, and several angels clasped their hands in front of their chests.

"That'll hold them for a few minutes. It's a pretty long song for a reason," Gabriel said. He put out his cigar on the rock wall and stashed it underneath his halo, behind his ear. "Listen. Jamie. I have to go inside for a moment to check on Mary. You wait here. You'll be okay." Gabriel let go of Jamie's hand and turned to go. She immediately felt the chill of the night air through her thin nightgown.

"Oh, Gabriel!" Jamie cried. "Don't leave me alone, please? Can I come with you? *Please?* You said you'd never leave me behind. You *promised*!"

Gabriel regarded her a long while. His eyes were the youngest and the strongest and gentlest eyes Jamie had ever looked into. It was hard for her not to look away, but she was frightened that he would leave her again.

Then Gabriel sighed, and smiled just a little. "I guess I did, didn't I?" He offered his arm like an escort. "Well, all right, child. But hold on tight to me. You'll be invisible as long as you do. And no talking. Remember where you are. The baby is only about half-an-hour old, and his parents don't need extra stress right now."

"I'll be good," she said, and gasped. "I can see through my arms!" She looked at Gabriel and was surprised to be able to see all the way through him, too.

"*Duh*," Gabriel mimicked her voice perfectly. "Come on, let's you and I go take a quick peek." Gabriel gently tugged Jamie's arm, and they began to walk deeper under the canopy.

Jamie could see the canopy up close now. It was constructed of round, rough-cut logs. Several of the posts still had twigs on them, and a few leaves. The braces were tied together with leather straps, and the top was covered with straw. A two-pronged wooden pitchfork leaned against the rock wall. Underneath the canopy, Jamie could look back into the dark entrance of the grotto. She couldn't see anything, but as they entered the shadows, she began to hear movement—and voices.

"Jamie could see Mary over her shoulder in the dim light."

CHAPTER 7

CANDLE – GLOW

As Gabriel and Jamie entered the dark grotto, all of Jamie's senses became clearer. She could see movement, but only the shadows of forms. She heard a soft but urgent voice. The voice said, "*Hurry!*"

Jamie heard the stamping of hooves, the low snorts of horses, and the short bray of a donkey. And as Gabriel drew her nearer, she smelled the animal sweat and droppings, and another pungent smell, like a wound smells before it gets bandaged.

They stood inside the mouth of the grotto, and Jamie's eyes began to adjust. She could see two mangers. One was full of hay nearer the animals. The other was full of hay, too, but that one had a dark bundle on top. She could see steam rising from it. The bundle wriggled just a tiny bit, and Jamie heard one short whimper which ended in a rising sound, like a question.

Mary lay on a bed of straw among a pile of darkened rags and leather straps on the other side of the manger. Jamie could not see her well in the darkness, but she could see that Mary was wearing only a thin sleeveless shirt, and steam was coming from her, too. Mary had her arms folded tightly across her chest for warmth.

A deep voice came from farther back in the shadows. "I have no more to give him."

"It is not enough, Joseph!" Mary said, her voice quivering with cold. "He's shivering! See if there are any rags by the horses. Hurry!"

"I am looking. If only we had a candle. Wait! Here is something. It's cloth," Joseph said.

"Praise God!" Mary said.

"But they are filthy!" Joseph answered.

"My cloak will keep him clean, Joseph. Wrap the rags tight around him."

"But what about you, my love?"

"I'll be all right," Mary said, shivering worse now. "Tend to the baby first."

Joseph emerged from the darkness carrying an armful of rags. He was bearded and dressed almost the same as the shepherd boys, except that his legs were bare. Jamie wondered whether the darkened rags near Mary had once been Joseph's leggings.

Joseph gently wrapped the moving bundle and rocked it awhile, making clicking sounds with his tongue until the baby inside made a happy sound. Then he gently laid the bundle back into the manger. There was the faintest angel-glow around the head of the bundle. But maybe it was just Jamie's eyes adjusting to the light, because every time she tried to look directly at it, the glow disappeared from her view.

Joseph went quickly to Mary. "You're freezing!" he said and sat behind her, holding her in his arms. Again came the clicking sounds from his tongue.

"They don't have *anything*," Jamie said.

"That's right," Gabriel whispered back, and then held a finger to his lips.

"But how will they get by?" Jamie asked a little too loudly.

"Wait and see. Now *shush*." Gabriel held his finger up again, and then made his zipping-the-lip motion.

"Who's there?" Joseph said in a loud voice. He stood up and moved silently in front of the manger, his feet wide apart. Jamie could see him better now. There was a line of gray in his beard, but the muscles on his bare arms and legs were thick and well defined. And Joseph's big hands were balled into fists. Jamie was very thankful that she was invisible.

Jamie heard voices and footsteps behind her. Two boys approached, out of breath. They were older than John, but younger than Jacob and dressed the same, with sheepskin leggings. They came inside the grotto. Their breath sounded harsh and left clouds of fog. They stopped just inches from Jamie without seeing her.

"We saw angels!" the younger boy panted. "They told us to come here."

"It is true!" the older boy said, and dropped to his knees. "This baby must be the one of prophesy."

Joseph relaxed his fists and sighed. "I have been told that this is so," he said, and then returned to Mary. He did what he could to hold her against his warmth, but he too was coatless. He rubbed Mary's arms vigorously and kissed the top of her head. In the darkness, Jamie could hear Mary's breath, ragged with chill.

The older boy began to unstrap his sandals. "I have nothing to give the baby, but put these on the mother's legs," he said, and handed Joseph his own sheepskin leggings.

"I have something!" The younger boy pulled a lump from his waistband. "It's bread. I'm sorry it's mostly crust left. But it's all I have." He gave it to Joseph.

"It's a blessing just as it is," Mary said. "You are good boys. I will teach my son to be as kind as you."

Another shepherd boy about John's age ran into the entrance of the grotto and gasped. "It's true, father! Come and see!"

A man entered behind the boy and stood silently, his eyes wide and his breath steaming. After a moment, he said, "I brought fresh goat's milk."

"I don't have anything to give." The young boy looked sad, but suddenly brightened. "Wait! I have a piece of cheese! You can have it." The cheese crumbled in his hand as he gave it to Joseph.

"Thank you," Joseph said.

Another boy even younger than John appeared at the entrance, but did not enter. "*Eww*," he said, his nose wrinkling up. "It smells even worse than *sheep* in there!"

A deep, resonant voice spoke from farther outside. "Perhaps this will help, little one." Jamie turned and saw a man dressed even finer than Gaspar, his head covered with a cone-shaped hat with jewels in it. The man stepped forward. He carried with him at arm's length a golden bowl suspended by a golden chain. A pungent smoke rose from the bowl.

"Frankincense is the aroma of kings at times such as these," the richly dressed man said. "I have come far to give this gift to the one who will be the Messiah. A moving star led me to you." He swung the bowl about in the darkness, and a sharp tang filled Jamie's nostrils. It smelled a little like her dad's hot spiced cider.

Two more faces appeared at the Grotto's entrance. They were boys who looked alike, both a few years younger than Jacob. "I can't see anything," one of the boys said.

"Wait, I have a candle and flint," the other said. He left, and after a few moments returned carrying a lighted candle. He handed the candle to Joseph, who placed it at the head of the manger, directly in front of Mary's face. Its flickering light illuminated the grotto, and Jamie could finally see Mary. Jamie almost gasped out loud but put her hand over her mouth instead. Mary was just a young girl. She couldn't be very much older than her sister Lindsey.

Mary's face was dark with dust and grime. But though she was shivering, she was smiling. "Thank you! Thank you all," she said.

Jamie felt ashamed. She had always had so much; she could not remember wanting anything and not getting it, and still she had wanted more. Yet here was a girl who had nothing, and was thankful for dirty rags and a single crust of bread. She remembered that Gabriel had asked her earlier if she could imagine that, and she couldn't. She had considered the shepherds to be poor people, and yet they had given freely of what little they had. She wished that she too had something to give, but she had nothing with her, except… Jamie looked at Mary, who sat shivering, her eyes closed against the cold.

At that moment, Gabriel pulled against her arm and motioned with his head toward the entrance. "Time to leave," he whispered in her ear. They moved silently toward the grotto entrance.

"Wait!" Jamie cried, resisting his pull. "I have something I have to do." Gabriel's grip on her arm was firm as he gazed into her eyes, but Jamie stared straight back and said, *"Please!"*

Gabriel's grip relaxed a little, but remained on Jamie's arm. "Jamie, angels mustn't interfere," he said.

"But I'm not an angel! I'm a little girl!" Jamie tried to break free, but it was like trying to pry off a part of herself. *"Please*, Gabriel! *I have to do this!"*

Gabriel regarded her with his strong, kind, ageless eyes, and finally let go of her hand. "All right. But come right back out," he said.

Jamie's glow began to dim, and she could no longer see through her arms. She began to feel the bitter cold of the night air again, but was determined to do what she had decided to do. She walked quickly to Mary's side and placed her precious cuddly around Mary's shoulders. As Jamie pulled it together in front of Mary and let go, the blanket instantly stopped shimmering and returned to its original color, sky blue.

Mary sighed and pulled the blanket tightly around herself. "It's still warm," she said, and smiled.

"Expect others like myself," the richly dressed man was talking to Joseph. "I know of at least two, possibly three, who have followed the star. I did not expect to be the first." He handed the golden bowl to Joseph. "You can sell this for food and shelter in the morning."

"Bless you," Mary said, her voice steady now. "Bless you all!" Mary then looked directly into Jamie's eyes, and a warmth spread over Jamie in spite of the cold. "You are all so kind," Mary added. Pale wet lines streaked down from her eyes. "How can we repay you?"

"Your son will find a way," the rich man said.

"Are you a magus?" Jamie asked him.

"I have been called such by others," the magus said.

"I met a magus on the way here," Jamie said. "His name was Gaspar."

"I don't see how this can be true," the magus said.

A voice from nowhere, or possibly from outside, said, *"Jamie—shhh!"*

"It is *so* true!" Jamie said. "I talked to him. He's going to be late. He took a wrong turn and went to Jerusalem."

"This cannot be true!" the magus exclaimed.

Again the invisible voice: *"Jamie! Zip!"*

"Gaspar was very sad. He was bringing myrrh," Jamie said. The wise man gasped and put a hand over his mouth. "Listen," Jamie continued. "Gaspar is going to want you to go to Jerusalem with him. Don't go. A bad man lives there…"

"Jamie! Enough!" The voice was loud and heard everywhere at once, followed by a cough and several disgusting old-man noises.

"I couldn't help it," Jamie cried. "It happened on accident!"

Mary sat up into a kneeling position by the manger, her new blanket wrapped tightly around her. "Gabriel? Is that you?" Mary asked, looking around into the shadows. "I'd know those sounds anywhere. Are you here?"

"Now and always, Mary," Gabriel said. He appeared slowly, glowing pale and translucent, his wings full and new, and he himself looking centuries younger. As he drew near to Mary, she smiled and reached out to him, but he stopped and pulled back. "Do not touch me, Mary. You need to stay completely in *this* world for now," he said, but he was smiling tenderly.

"*You* have arranged all this kindness, haven't you?" Mary said. "I should have known."

"*Me?*" Gabriel drew his hands innocently to his chest. "What, crumbly cheese, a dog-bitten blanket, and an old used candle?" Gabriel took his cigar from behind his ear, glanced at the baby in the manger, and then put it back behind his ear again. "Girl, if it were up to me, I'd have given you all of Greece. Better climate. Better horses. Better cheese. This? Me? No, not much of it. Maybe a little." Gabriel held up a finger and thumb close together.

"Bless you, Gabriel," Mary said. A large feather popped out on Gabriel's right wing. Another smaller one popped out of his left nostril. "D-word," Gabriel said and plucked the smaller one away.

"And bless you, too," Mary said to Jamie.

Jamie felt a twinge along both of her shoulder blades, and two large white feathers popped out of her back. When she shrugged her shoulders, they moved like wings. "*Cool*!" Jamie said.

Gabriel turned to Mary. "You and Joseph have done very well. I'm very fond of both of you. I have to leave you now for a little while, but you'll have a few angels to look out for you. Are you ready for visitors?"

"Yes, all right," Mary said. "But just a few."

"Thank you," Gabriel sighed. "Don't worry. Like most angels, you won't even know they're here. I have a not-so-little girl to take home now, but I'll be back before you know I'm gone. Angel flight is like that." Gabriel turned his eyes to Jamie. "Come, Jamie," he said.

"Good bye, Mary," Jamie said.

Gabriel looked at Jamie. "We don't hear that term in heaven much. Is that short for *God-be-with-you*? I like that. Maybe I'll use it now and then."

"God be with you," Mary said to Jamie.

"We have to go now, child." Gabriel took Jamie's hand, and immediately they both turned translucent again. "Good bye," he said the same as Jamie had said it, and smiled at Mary. Gabriel carefully tucked his magnificent new wings as he turned toward the entrance.

Gabriel pulled Jamie along after him so rapidly that she barely had time to look over her shoulder. But as she did, she managed to see Mary kneeling by the manger as she pulled the sky-blue blanket up over her head. Joseph stood at her side. Shepherds were kneeling by the animals, and the wise man stood by the wall. A glow from the manger lit the entire room. Jamie was just wondering whether the glow had been from the candle or from something else when Gabriel reached the opening of the grotto, and they both exited into the bright glow from thousands and thousands of caroling angels.

"A *few* angels?" Jamie said to Gabriel.

"Well, the number sixteen million might have alarmed her. Besides, it's God's will that they all stay invisible. Not to mention, what He can do with time," Gabriel answered. He held up his peculiar trumpet and blew the last few notes of the *Hallelujah Chorus* just as it ended.

"All right, everything is ready!" Gabriel said in his everywhere-at-once voice. **"Four at a time. Remain invisible,"** Gabriel said to cheers and applause. He belched almost as loud as his everywhere-at-once voice. **"Sorry,"** he said.

Gabriel put away his trumpet and turned toward Jamie to say something else, but before he could speak, a young boy ran between them. It was John, the shepherd boy. He was carrying a furry sheepskin that was so large, he had trouble seeing in front of himself. He knocked Jamie's and Gabriel's hands apart, and Jamie instantly became solid again. Just then, Jacob came running up to the entrance too. He was also carrying a sheepskin, but he was bigger and could see fine.

"Hello, Jacob," Jamie said and shrugged her shoulders at him, making her two new feathers move like a butterfly drying its wings. "How's Dog?" she said.

Jacob fainted.

"Time to go home, child," Gabriel said and gently took her hand again. The two of them began to glow very brightly, and Jamie felt herself rising above the ground.

Gabriel disappeared into a huge cloud of smoke.

CHAPTER 8

A HORSE RIDE

The canopy and then the hill shrank away below them as Gabriel and Jamie rose higher and higher. Gabriel's strong new wings worked beautifully, and they surged far upward with each flap. Gabriel, however, was neither strong nor new, and soon he was too tired to do anything but make feeble little flaps while hovering and gasping for breath.

Jamie looked upward toward the Christmas star. It was still too far away to appear as anything other than a star. Angels streamed down from it, four abreast in a straight line past them, singing and chanting as they descended. A few angels even passed them going upwards toward the star.

"Great music, Gabe!" some of the upward-bound angels called.

Gabriel just gave them the thumbs-up sign while he panted.

One angel, who looked surprisingly young to have such long grey hair, zoomed up very close. "Gabriel!" he said, grinning.

"You did good, George Frederick," Gabriel said, still gasping for breath. The young angel with the grey hair did a cartwheel and sped upward into the night.

"Who was that?" Jamie asked.

"Handel," Gabriel replied in between pants.

Jamie inhaled quickly. "You mean, *the* Handel, as in Handel's *Messiah*, the guy who wrote it?"

"I wrote it," Gabriel said. "Handel just took notes. I told you, I've been working on this night for a long time." Gabriel coughed and then made a particularly disgusting sound to clear his throat.

"You ought to quit smoking," Jamie said. "It's bad for you."

"It's okay, I don't inhale." Gabriel coughed, and followed it with a long wheeze.

Just as he ended the wheeze, Jamie heard a *"ping"* sound, and one of Gabriel's new feathers arced back and forth as it fell away into the darkness.

"Sure," Jamie said, frowning at him.

"It's the night air, it tightens me up," Gabriel said. Immediately, one more of his feathers made a *"ping"* sound and fell away; there was a big new blank space in his left wing.

"See what you get for making excuses?" Jamie said.

"I know, I know," Gabriel said, still a little short of breath, but recovering now. "Listen. I promise I'll quit right after Christmas."

"Hey, wait a minute," Jamie frowned. "Didn't you say that in heaven, every night is Christmas Eve? It's *never* going to be after Christmas."

"Ping, ping," went two more feathers. Gabriel had a brand new blank place in his right wing now.

"I'm cutting down," Gabriel said. *"Ping"* went another feather. "I don't want to talk about it," he added, grimacing as though expecting to lose another. He didn't that time. "God is so *sensitive*," he muttered.

"Ping."

"*And* we're lucky to have Him," Gabriel added quickly, trying to smile. After Gabriel had rested long enough to catch his breath a bit, Jamie took Gabriel's hand in both of hers. "Gabriel?" she said.

"Yeah, what?"

"I'm sorry I talked too much."

"You didn't talk too much," Gabriel said. "But you might have if I hadn't stopped you."

"I didn't say too much? *Whew!*" Jamie sighed. "That's good, because sometimes I say things and then I think, *duh!*" Jamie tapped her forehead with her palm.

Gabriel laughed. "It's okay, Kiddo. Nothing a little editing can't fix in the next couple of centuries. Actually, you did good." Gabriel retrieved his cigar from behind his ear, beneath his halo. He put it into his mouth and then lit it on his halo without using his hands. "Tell your dad thanks for reading to you. I always like the educated trips best." Gabriel coughed. "But I knew you'd do good. That's why I took you. I've been putting the pieces of this night together like a three thousand year old puzzle."

"I thought it was only two thousand years," Jamie said.

"Hah! A lot more work than that!" Gabriel huffed. "All that planning and prophesy! I used to think that being archangel was hard. Being Mary's guardian is a lot harder, let me tell you. Long hours. Not nearly enough beauty rest." Gabriel shrugged his shoulders, moving gently up and down as he did so.

"Well," Jamie said, "I'm glad I didn't talk too much. I thought maybe I'd ruined things for you. And then, when I got to heaven for real, the first thing I'd have to say is, like, *I'm sorry*, and God is like *this* at me." Jamie made an angry scowl-face at Gabriel.

"Ooo, that *would* be scary," Gabriel said. "But try not to get too far ahead of yourself, Kiddo. God isn't like that."

"Well, what's He like, then?" Jamie asked. "Can we go by the pearly gates so I can peek in?"

Gabriel laughed, more like a snort, really. "What, you think you'll get to see God? Maybe see some old geezer with a nice beard? Maybe wearing a pointy hat with stars and moons on it, or better yet, a long white robe? Maybe he'll be out working in the garden along heaven's fence, and you could lean in and say, 'How's it goin', God? *Yo*, nice job on roses!'"

"Yeah, well, *maybe*," Jamie said.

"Well, God isn't like that," Gabriel said again. "I mean, He can be if you need Him to be, hey, no problem." Gabriel held up both of his hands apologetically. "But God is much more than that, too."

"Like how?" Jamie asked.

"Well, let's see…how can I…*hmm*." Gabriel absently took several puffs on his cigar, and then began coughing repeatedly until he was out of breath. He made a disgusting throat-clearing sound, and then shook his head. "Maybe I do need to quit smoking. Maybe Michael's right; I'm too old for this gig. Do I look *pale* to you?"

Before she could answer that all angels looked pale to her, Jamie heard the rapid clatter of hooves. A group of men dressed in cowboy clothes came riding up with spare horses.

A large cowboy wearing a leather vest and a red bandanna sideways around his neck took off his hat and wiped his brow with his sleeve. "You call for horses, pilgrim?" the cowboy said.

"No," Gabriel huffed.

"I could have swore…" the cowboy said.

"Well, ain't that a dang shame," a thin cowboy with dark wavy hair said. "We hadda go all the way to Greece for these! What're we gonna do with 'em now?"

"Greece? Oh," Gabriel remembered. "Maybe I did, but it was a' accident."

"Well, when there's horses, might as well ride, pilgrim!" The first cowboy handed Jamie a set of reins.

"Me? I don't know how to ride a horse!" Jamie cowered under the pale white horse's head which towered over her. That was when she noticed the horse had an enormous pair of wings.

"Don't worry, little lady. They got good horses in Greece. Awful hard to rope though. Sorry we're late," the cowboy said. "Mount up, pilgrims! Let's ride!"

The two cowboys were joined by other mounted men whose faces Jamie recognized from watching old westerns on TV with her dad, but she didn't remember any of their names. They helped her and Gabriel up onto the backs of the two winged horses.

As the horses spread their wings, Gabriel's grip pulled away from Jamie's hand.

"Gabriel!" Jamie shouted.

"It's okay, Jamie. Your horse is an angel, too. As long as you're touching him, you'll be fine. In fact, it's perfect. Watch *this*!" Gabriel grinned and blew an enormous smoke ring. When the smoke cleared, Gabriel, his horse, and all of the other riders were gone. Jamie was all alone on the back of a giant, snorting, winged horse.

"Gabriel? Are you there? Gabriel?" Jamie could hear a little tremor in her own voice, but she struggled to remain brave. "Gabriel! I know you're there. You said you wouldn't leave me. Would you? *Gabriel?* I know he's here," she said, holding onto her horse's mane so tight her hand hurt.

Jamie heard coughing, and Gabriel and his winged horse flashed into view a little clearer with every cough.

"Course I'm here, Kiddo. Relax, I never left you."

"You scare me sometimes. I was feeling lost!"

"*Tsk, tsk*, naughty word, naughty word! But I didn't mean to scare you. It's just that you asked. God is like that. If you stop trying so hard to *see* Him, you'll start to feel His presence around you all the time. You see, Jamie, God is any place love and kindness are. God is in every mother's loving kiss, or father's protective arm around a shoulder. God is in every hand that reaches out to help the sick, or feed the hungry, or give shelter to the cold. God is in every gift given freely from the heart. In fact, all paths to God begin with caring about others. This is what that little baby's message is going to be all about—that, and to let us know that you can actually get from there to here. And you helped in your own way to bring it about, Jamie."

"I did? How?"

"By giving your most precious possession to someone who needed it more. You and the others, the shepherds and the magi, all showed great kindness. That will be passed on as a lifelong lesson to a special little boy. You did very good, Kiddo. Two feathers good!"

"Can I keep them?" Jamie imagined showing up in third grade sporting her new one-feather wings.

"We'll see. You're not an official angel yet," Gabriel said, more relaxed now. "No doubt lots of paperwork, don't you know," he added.

"*Jeez*, have I got something for show-and-tell!" She exclaimed, hunching her shoulders up and down and looking over them to see her feathers move.

Gabriel laughed. "Jeez—is that short for Jesus? I like that. I'm gonna start saying that. Jeez," he chuckled.

They neared the star and joined a line waiting to go back the other way. A big red light over the gate turned green. Michael, still standing in all his splendor just inside the doorway, blew his same two notes.

Gabriel and Jamie looked at each other and said exactly at the same time, "Boring!"

Gabriel took his trumpet out of his sash, and played a lively marching song. He finished just as the two of them arrived at the gate. But they couldn't get through because Michael's horn suddenly barred their way.

"Traffic change," Michael said. "Sorry. But I did want to speak with you, Gabriel."

"What?" Gabriel sounded impatient even to Jamie. Maybe he was just tired.

"I just wanted to ask how the nativity is shaping up. I think the music is going well." Michael grinned, a wan, royal kind of grin.

"Fine, your wingship. Just dandy. A classic. Ready for final editing." Gabriel sighed. "Thank God I'm almost done."

Michael clapped his hands, his humongous wings pulling his wing-bearers off balance as he did so. "Oh, I knew it! I *knew* I'd given the best gift of all!"

Gabriel's mouth dropped open and his cigar fell out, but he caught it in mid-air. *"You?"* Gabriel's brow slowly furrowed into a brewing storm. *"You've* given the best gift of all? I've given three thousand years of diligence, from prophesy to fulfillment. I've given hundreds, no, thousands of angels their personal revelations. I've prepared the time and the place. I brought all of them together—Mary and Joseph, the shepherds, the magi, and not a single sheep was lost. I have muck and mire all over my robe to prove it. I've blown my horn 'til my cheeks have stretch marks. I've wrestled with kings, and tumbled from the sky so many times—why, look at my wings! I've lost more feathers over Christmas than you've had your whole career, you young upstart! What in God's name have *you* given to Christmas?"

Gabriel put his cigar back into his mouth, clamped his teeth down on it, and glowered at Michael. Gabriel looked exactly the same to Jamie as he had when the crude bearded man had lifted him off the ground.

Michael's eyebrows raised a little bit. "Why Gabriel, I gave *you*." Gabriel's mouth dropped open again, but no words came out, just a few coughs and sputters. It was the only time Jamie ever saw the old angel with nothing to say.

Michael grinned his royal grin again and spun around to face the crowd bunching up at the gate. As he turned, his wings swept aside everything in their path, wing-bearers and angels alike, missing the horses by inches.

"Behold, the Christmas angel, in whom I am well pleased!" Michael said to whoever might be listening; they certainly could hear him well enough. The horn in Michael's outstretched arm pointed straight at Gabriel, the bell of it directly under his chin.

"Who does he think he is, anyway?" Gabriel frowned. Then he looked at Jamie and smiled. He took a big puff from his cigar and said, "You know what, Jamie? I've decided to quit smoking after all." He dropped his cigar stub down the bell of the archangel Michael's horn as he dismounted from his winged horse. "Gotta leave the horses behind, Kiddo. People abandon them in-between, and they're too stupid to find their way out."

Gabriel helped Jamie down, and then gave the horses a pat on the forehead. "Thanks, Peg. You were a good ride. Go home now." Gabriel whispered in his ear, and the great winged horses galloped off.

When Michael blew his horn for the next traffic change, only one flat, muffled note came out. He scowled at Gabriel. There was thunder and lightning as several of Gabriel's feathers fell out. Gabriel again looked almost as bedraggled as Jamie's statue of him.

"Gotta go!" Gabriel grinned, grabbed Jamie's hand, and jerked her through the gate.

"*Whoa*," Jamie said, just as hundreds of singing and laughing angels flew all around them, sweeping them along inside their wing-wake.

"**I'll remember this, Gabriel!**" Michael shouted over the thunder, his voice heard everywhere at once again.

"He's so good at that part," Gabriel whispered in Jamie's ear.

"Gabriel," Jamie said, "I have a question."

"Okay, but make it quick. We need to get you home."

"How come you put your cigar down Michael's horn? Didn't you say that angels were supposed to be nice to one another?" Jamie said.

"Well, child, it's kind of like being a parent. Sometimes the best thing to do doesn't seem nice right away. But in the long run, it's still the best thing. Now, you take Michael for instance. He's got a lot of responsibility, what with running everything in-between heaven and earth and all. But sometimes he gets a little bit big-winged, the angels say. You know, thinking he's hot stuff. I know I shouldn't think poorly of him, but, well, you ought to be able to do your job and still not see yourself as better than the rest of us. That's what I think. Anyways, everybody needs someone in their life to keep them humble. With Michael, that's my job. Understand?"

Jamie wrinkled up her nose at the thought. "I don't think so."

"Well, you'll understand humility a whole lot better when you grow up and get married." Gabriel chuckled quietly. "But never mind, child. Just keep a loving heart through it all and you'll be fine." Gabriel gave Jamie a little hug, the kind her dad had given her on Christmas Eve.

Gabriel's hug reminded Jamie that her dad had given her the old angel statue for Christmas, and she missed her home and family. She took Gabriel's hand in both of hers. "Gabriel, let's go home," she said.

"Yes, it's time," he answered.

The angels thinned out as they flew in all different directions, still laughing and singing. But Gabriel and Jamie slowly drifted to a stop.

"Why are we stopping?" Jamie asked.

"Lack of direction, probably," Gabriel said.

"I thought you were taking me home."

"I can't take you home. The in-between place doesn't work that way. You have to take yourself home," Gabriel said.

Jamie looked around. All she could see were a few small circles of light moving away from them, and some stars twinkling off in the far distance. "But Gabriel, I don't know where I am! I told you, I'm *tired*, and I'm *lost*!"

She felt a tear coming, but wiped it away with the back of her hand before it became an actual drop. That way she could tell herself she wasn't actually crying.

Gabriel gently put his arm around her. "Listen. Jamie. We don't use the L-word in heaven because we don't have to. I told you, we travel by desire. All you have to do is wish to be home, and you'll be on your way there."

"I wish to be home," Jamie said.

A tiny star blinked in the distance. It shined bright for a moment, and then quickly disappeared.

"Wait, *wait*," Gabriel said. "I don't really care what you think God looks like, Kiddo. But if you want to get any closer than a bazillion miles out, at least you could say *please*." He gave Jamie a gentle hug. "Remember your basics, Kiddo. Please. Thank you. You're welcome. It was good enough advice for King David. It's good advice for you, too."

"Gabriel, will King David ever get his wings?" Jamie asked.

"Oh my, yes," Gabriel chuckled. "He's a good boy in his heart. He's just a bit willful, and the stubborn ones take longer, sometimes. But I don't doubt that in four or five millennia, David will be first in line for archangel." Gabriel muttered something under his breath which sound to Jamie very much like, *"He's got the attitude already."*

"*Ping*," went another feather in Gabriel's right wing as it fell away.

"Drat!" Gabriel said.

Jamie laughed out loud at Gabriel's mock frustration. "Gabriel, I have another question," she said.

"Make it quick. I've had a *long* day," Gabriel said.

"When we get home, are you going to be just a statue again?"

"I was never just a statue, any more than you were ever just a photograph. When we get home, you'll be getting up on Christmas morning, and I'll be back in Bethlehem looking after Mary on Christmas Eve. Just a few more minor details to go."

"Will I get to see you next Christmas Eve?" Jamie asked.

"Sorry," Gabriel replied. "Only one trip per customer."

"Will I *ever* get to see you again?" Jamie gave the old angel a fierce hug, at least as much of him as her arms could reach around.

"'Course you will, in about…" Gabriel glanced at his duct-taped hourglass. "Wait, I looked that up before, didn't I? *Jeez*, I'm starting to repeat myself! I really should retire again. I could just be done. I could be done, if God weren't such a perfectionist!"

"*Ping.*"

"*And* we're lucky to have Him," Gabriel forced a smile upwards into the air.

Gabriel, I want to go home now," Jamie said. The star blinked on again, twinkled brightly twice this time, and then went out.

"Then say the words like you mean them, Kiddo. Set your heart afire with them!"

Jamie held her hands together the way she had seen Gabriel do it. She closed her eyes and said, "*Please*, God, I want to be home again."

Jamie pictured her room so clearly in her mind that she could see all her bears across from her bed. She tried to remember their names. *Sailor-Bear, and Yum-yum*, she thought...

Suddenly, the two of them were spinning through a huge stone-lined tunnel toward a bright light. They twisted and tumbled, almost like falling, only upwards. Jamie could see feathers flying everywhere. She felt twinges in both her shoulder blades. "Gabriel!" she shouted, hanging onto him with all her might.

Then they fell into the light, and Jamie couldn't see anything more at all.

Get up, Dork! It's Christmas morning!

CHAPTER 9

CHRISTMAS MORNING

"Gabriel!" Jamie cried and squeezed as hard as she could. Something soft gave way, and feathers filled the air above her. The blinding light went out and then came on again. She squinted at it and discovered that it was only her bedroom ceiling light. She was back in her own bed again, and she found herself hugging a pillow with a brand new rip in the side. Feathers floated down from everywhere, settling on her head and face. Her two brand new wing feathers were gone. Jamie felt surprised and a little bit disoriented. She blew a feather off her nose.

"Get up, dork!" Lindsey stood at her bedroom door with her hand on the light switch. "It's

Christmas morning! Mom's home, and she brought more presents!" Jamie's ceiling light went off and on again. "Hubba chop!" Lindsey said.

Jamie looked around her room. Home again. Everything looked *almost* the same, like things looked when you came home from a long vacation, she thought. Her teddy-bears were all in a line, her Barbies were both in their little beds. She spotted Gabriel sitting on her night-stand, exactly as he had been the night before. She picked up the old angel statue and tucked it under her arm as she swung her feet out of bed. "Thanks for everything, Gabe," she said, but, of course, the little wooden statue didn't answer.

Jamie put on a bathrobe and ran to the living room where her family was waiting for her. She paused at the doorway to take in the whole of it— the twinkling lights, the stockings hanging heavy with goodies, the scent of fir needles and bayberry candles, the smell of hot-spiced cider, which now reminded her of frankincense. Her dad was sipping from his cup by the fireplace, wearing his bathrobe. Lindsey had hers on, too. The only one dressed was Jamie's mom, who was still wearing her white nurse's uniform and her plain white shoes. But she was holding two big colored boxes with ribbons on them. Jamie's mom bent down and placed the boxes under the tree.

"Merry Christmas, Jamie," her mom said. "My, it's good to be home!"

"*Sure is!*" Jamie exclaimed. Her mother gave her a puzzled look.

"Come on, dork!" Lindsey said, taking her Christmas stocking from its nail below the mantle. "I swear, you walk like a little flower girl in a wedding. Well, I'm not waiting for *you!*" Lindsey dumped her stocking in the middle of the floor, sat down, and began poring through the pile of candy canes, finger toys, puzzles, and fruit bars.

Jamie walked up to the nativity scene, where her dad had just given his new angel mobile a spin. The little glass angels that had fallen off the tree now circled around over the top of the manger, suspended from almost invisible fish-line. The new angel mobile hung down from the ceiling in an ever widening spiral. "Oh, Daddy, it's beautiful!" Jamie said.

"Like it?" her dad took a sip from his steaming cider.

"You got it just right," Jamie said. She looked at the cardboard stable with the nativity scene inside, and it was just as she remembered it. Mary was kneeling by the manger, wearing a blue cloak over her head. Joseph was standing beside her, wearing his long cinnamon-colored shirt. The baby was wrapped in swaddling clothes, or cloth, as Gabriel had insisted. Shepherds knelt nearby (with the three legged sheep leaning up against a rock), and the wise-men stood with their camels. Jamie stepped closer and peered in at Mary.

"Dad?" Jamie said. "Has Mary always been blue?"

"I think so. Tradition has always pictured Mary as dressed in blue. Why?"

"Speaking of blue," Jamie's mom said, "where's your cuddly this morning?"

Jamie stood on her toes so that she could get her face as close to the nativity scene as possible. She could see Mary clearly. Mary must have also been dropped sometime in the past. The little figure had a crack in it, and a tiny piece of her sky-blue cloak was broken away. A corner.

Jamie smiled. "Oh, I found a use for it," she said. "I won't be needing it anymore."

"Let's open presents!" Lindsey shouted.

"Just a minute," Jamie said. She reached up and placed her statue beside the nativity scene. "I think the Christmas angel would like to be close to Mary," she added.

Jamie's dad glanced at her with a strange look on his face. "I think so, too," he said after a pause.

"Hey, dork-meister! Stop playing with your dolls, and let's get to ripping!" Lindsey said.

"That's right," Jamie's mom said. She took a last sip of her coffee, then set her cup down quickly. "I just can't wait any longer to give you your present, Jamie." She handed Jamie one of the large colored boxes she had been carrying when Jamie had come into the room.

Jamie broke the ribbon and opened the box in record time. It was the very lap-top computer that she had so desperately wanted. "Oh, Mom! It's beautiful! It's just what I wanted!" she exclaimed. She opened it up and turned it on.

"Cool! Lindsey said. "Where's mine? Where's mine, Mom? Dad?" Lindsey began sorting through the boxes under the tree in a not-so-dainty manner while Jamie's mom and dad looked at each other.

"I'm sorry, Lindsey," her mom said. "I just didn't know you wanted one. And anyway, they're frightfully expensive."

"What a rip!" Lindsey said with her mouth remaining open. Lindsey sat up into the tree branches, knocking the lights askew, and looking for all the world like she had just eaten the wrong kind of olive. "How come the dork-meister gets one and I don't? I could have used one way more than her. I have tons of homework. It's not *fair*!" Lindsey said.

"We got something else for you, Lindsey," her dad said.

A tiny piece of Mary's blue cloak had broken away—a corner.

"Sure," Lindsey muttered. Her mouth snapped shut and her lower lip pushed out almost as far as her nose.

Jamie thought about all the times Lindsey had talked to her about doing their homework on computers, and how cool a lap-top would be. It had been Lindsey who had first showed her the advertisement about that very model. And it was true that Lindsey had tons more homework than she did. Jamie sighed, turned off the lap-top, and closed its cover. She walked over and set the tiny computer onto Lindsey's lap. "Here. You probably *can* use it more than I can," she said.

Lindsey's mouth dropped open again. "What are you *doing*?" she said.

"You use it first for awhile, and then you can show me how it works," Jamie said.

"Are you sure?" Lindsey's nose was wrinkled up so far that it made her eyes squint.

"Sure I'm sure. We'll just *share* it," Jamie said.

"Jeez-o-leez, thanks, Sis!" Lindsey said. Maybe she had squinted too hard, because she had to wipe something out of her eye.

"You're welcome," Jamie said, remembering Gabe's advice.

"Thanks, and you're welcome? So we're having manners now? What a concept," their dad said, looking at his two daughters with widened eyes.

"But I'd like to do something for *you*, Sis," Lindsey said.

"Well, I like 'Sis' way better than dork," Jamie said.

"You got it." Lindsey gave Jamie the first hug she could ever remember getting from her sister. "No more dork-meister," Lindsey said.

"It looks like our little girls are growing up," Jamie's mom said to her dad.

"They can be little angels, sometimes," Jamie's dad replied. He gave his mobile another spin, smiling absently. Then he held his cup out in front of himself. "A toast to the real Christmas spirit," he added.

Jamie pulled a candy cane out of her Christmas stocking. She broke it in half and gave the straight part to Lindsey. Lindsey held her cider cup down in front of Jamie, who dunked her curved candy cane half in it. Then her mom held up her coffee,

Lindsey held up her cider, and Jamie held up her dripping candy cane curve.

"Merry Christmas!" they all said to each other.

"And merry Christmas Eve, too!" Jamie pointed her candy cane half at the statue on the mantle before she put it into her mouth.

"Whatever do you mean?" Jamie's mom looked puzzled.

"Yes. I'd like to know, too," Jamie's dad said, staring at Jamie with that strange look again.

"It's kind of sort of part of the Christmas story," Jamie said.

"Yes, well, *hmm*… Maybe we'll get that far next year," Jamie's dad sighed.

Jamie stretched up to be closer to her dad's ear. "*Gabe says to say hello,*" she whispered, and winked at him.

Jamie's dad's eyes went wide, and his mouth dropped open. He stared at Jamie, then at the Christmas angel, and then back at Jamie again. "You mean, *Gabriel*? You mean, you and he…?"

Jamie nodded, and her dad laughed and laughed.

the end

www.ingramcontent.com/pod-product-compliance
Lightning Source LLC
LaVergne TN
LVHW041813060526
838201LV00046B/1245